Outbreak
On The
Plains

By T.J. Judah

This is a work of fiction. It is not technically, medically or historically correct, nor is it intended to be. It is, in short, an adventure thriller. Any reference to persons living or deceased is strictly coincidental.

Outbreak on the Plains

T.J. Judah

Published by T.J. Judah, 2024.

OUTBREAK ON THE PLAINS

First edition. March 23, 2024.

Copyright © 2024 T.J. Judah.

ISBN: 979-8224990047

Written by T.J. Judah.

Dedicated to my family who lived through this with me.

Fine Editing

M.L.Judah

T. Zimmerman

Introduction

After their exploits in 'Cherry-1 A Combat Controllers Tale,' and 'Mystery of The Mist at Cyan Mountain.'

R.J. and Cherry are in their mid-lives and living it pretty normally. He, is continuing his engineering work at the electronics factory and She, at her children's clinic. They have a son, Douglas who is a Pre-Med Student in College, Molly and Kyle, the twins, are in high school and are currently into Animal Husbandry, they are both interested in opening a Large Animal Veterinary hospital.

They still live in RJ's hometown of Pine Creek, where he grew up with his parents Dan and Martha Jansen, and his siblings younger brother Tom and older sister Lanora.

Dan and Martha own and operate the Lazy J restaurant and are getting ready to retire. Tom is a flight instructor in Kansas City and Marsha his wife, is a now retired FBI Special Agent. They are considering opening a Private Detective Agency in Kansas City.

Lanora is married to Darren and they have two daughters. He works for an Oil field / Chemical company, she is a CPA, and owns and operates a large Accounting and Law firm in Pine Creek. Mandy, their youngest has gone off to culinary school and is preparing to take over owner and operator of the Lazy J Casual and Fine dining establishment. Lea received a journalism degree and is currently working at a small market TV station in Sparksdale. She has her eye on a large market position at a Kansas City TV station.

The town of Pine Creek is located in middle America and would be characterized as a sleepy sort of mundane no-nonsense community that has recently grown to a population of about thirty-five thousand people, give or take a few after College and High School graduations.

The peace and tranquility of this relatively unknown and unassuming community was about to change with the shock wave of an F-4 tornado that scorched the Northwest side of the county and clipped the County Fair grounds. It turned out to be one of a massive wave of tornadoes spawned across the Plains resulting from a Collison of Gulf moisture and a Super cell low pressure front.

No strangers to mysteries and challenges, the team of Jansen and Company must now unravel a new mystery caused by the 'Storm of the Century.' One that once again vaults them into another universe of problem solving.

The situation develops when a strange looking cloud begins to form over the County Fair Grounds, no one notices until the wind suddenly reaches hurricane velocity. What happens next is the rest of the story.

Chapter One

"Getting Ready for the Fair"

"Hey hon, what's up?" said Roy.

"It's your birthday and I wanted to give you something you always wanted," replied Cherry.

"Well, what is it?"

"Open it up and see."

She smiled and giggled in excitement.

He ripped open the package and stared at it in amazement.

"Oh my gosh. You found one, I can't believe it, you actually found one. It's absolutely beautiful. I knew they existed, but when I was a kid, I was working towards one goal, the Cherry-1. Wow, an authentic 'Roy Rogers' wrist watch. I'll never take it off. Thank you so much. This is great. And look it's engraved on the back. Roy...HBD...CJ. That is so cool."

"I knew from your mom that Roy Rogers was your TV hero. I never knew you were actually named after him."

"I didn't either until one day when I was about ten, she told me while we were watching Roy Rogers reruns on TV.

Ok down to business. Molly...Kyle...are you ready?"

"Yes dad, yes dad... came the echo."

"I'm going down to the pen to collect the critters. Molly's lamb and Kyle's calf. They've been pampered half to death for the past two weeks. I bet they're ready to see some action," said RJ.

RJ ambled on over to the special pens where the show animals are kept in pristine surroundings. Molly and Kyle have raised Champion livestock for three years running and hope this fourth year is going to win them scholarships to State University.

The stock trailer is small enough to carry two to four animals and is, as you might expect, spotless. The animals have been fed with only the finest grains money can buy.

The year is 1999 and it's time for the spring showing season.

RJ and the kids loaded into the truck; Cherry would come along later for the Awards Ceremony. They drove the few miles northwest to the new fairground located in the 900-acre wood. It was one of the good things that came about from the incident at Cyan Mountain.

RJ backed into the display corral. Kyle and Molly jumped out and opened the gate and unloaded their prize animals. They took them to their respective single pens where they would stay until show time.

RJ drove the truck and trailer to the far side of the parking area. It was especially crowded this year with the new high school opening last fall. Many of the local kids are getting into the Show Animal gig as it has begun to have some coveted benefits in terms of scholarships to big universities, and the prize money has increased substantially.

In spite of the stiff competition, the Jansen kids knew their stuff and had preselected animals that were of grade A breeding. They started off with a head start just from being able to acquire good stock to begin with.

The day dragged on. RJ went off to get them some lunch. He brought back some corndogs and drinks.

"Eat up kids, this is about as good as it gets at the County fair."

They watched intently as one group after another showed their animals and the scores began to pile up.

"Whew," said Molly. "There are some pretty good-looking lambs here today."

"And some fine-looking calves as well. No worries though...eh sis," said Kyle.

Finally, after hours of viewing it was their turn to show. First it was Molly's turn with 'Sweet Pea' her prized lamb. She stood there while the judges poked and prodded and smirked and grunted and sneered and wrote marks on the clipboards.

"Nice looking animal young lady," one judge quietly whispered.

Then it was Kyle's turn with 'Badger' his Hereford calf. The judges did the same for his animal, poked and prodded, smirked, sneered, and wrote on the clipboards.

"Hum...seen better," muttered one judge.

Kyle and Molly were both getting very nervous as the competition had been tough this year. RJ watched from the stands and sweated bullets. It was hard to tell from the judges' reactions what or who might have a lead in the standings. Cherry showed up just then and sat beside him.

"How's it going," she whispered.

"So far so good. There are a lot of nice-looking animals here today, from all over the state no less. The kids did really well, showing their animals. The judges are finalizing their scores right now. The Awards Ceremony is on at 5:00 P.M. sharp, or so they say.

Say, did you see the Smiths have a new litter of Shepard pups? They look really good. Do you think we could get one?"

Just then the kids and their animals began to line up across the giant corral for the awards ceremony. Kyle and Molly were next to each other, looking confident and proud of their work.

The announcer came on the loud speaker.

"Ladies and gentlemen, boys and girls. In the lamb competition, the sixth-place prize goes to ... the fifth place goes to ... fourth place and so on to first place goes to 'Sweet Pea' and Molly Jansen for the fourth year in a row. There was a huge round of applause and a few groans.

Somebody in the crowd mumbled, "she's unbeatable."

For the Calf division, sixth place goes to ...and so on down to first place...and first place goes to 'Badger' and Kyle Jansen. The Jansen kids ran and hugged each other and jumped up and down in fine celebratory fashion.

Somebody else in the crowd mumbled, "thank the Lord they're graduating this year."

Cherry and RJ greeted Molly and Kyle at the gate and got some hugs and began preparations for the bidding process.

"Cherry, I'm going to go get the truck and bring it around the back. You can watch and stay with the kids while the bidding goes on."

Both of the kids' animals received grade A endorsements and garnered top money, even better than last year. If they didn't get scholarships, it would be enough for the first year's tuition to university.

Cherry watched closely as the proceedings concluded. Everything turned out the way it should, she was satisfied with the outcomes.

"Where's dad, mom?" questioned Kyle.

"He went out to the parking lot to get the truck. He said it's quite a hike."

Just then the wind started whistling through the stock building. It grew stronger and debris started blowing through the open doors.

"Stay put everyone, there is a severe storm forming just to our southwest. It should pass by in a few moments."

Kyle, curious as a kid can be, stuck his head out the door just in time to see a huge funnel cloud pass just south of the fairgrounds and clip the edge of the parking lot.

"Oh my God," he shouted. "It's a gigantic tornado, it just passed over by where dad had parked the truck. I hope he got out of there in time!"

Molly screamed in terror as her ears were popping and debris was slamming into them.

Cherry tried to yell for them to get down but the sound of her voice was drowned out by the vicious wind. Suddenly, as fast as it had come up, it died down.

"Everyone OK?" she squealed.

"I think so," cried Molly.

"I'm OK mom," said Kyle.

They stood there taking account of themselves and watched as people began to gather and depart the area. Just then one of the out buildings collapsed, it had livestock and people inside. People started running for the building to rescue those people inside.

First responders started showing up. People were pulling debris away from the building. Cattle and people started coming out. Some were injured with cuts and bruises. The responders joined by anyone with gloves were yanking and pulling sheet metal and wood. They uncovered several of the show animals. A beam had fallen over the corral and trapped them but they were otherwise ok.

The fireman and sheriff's deputies called for ambulances and more help. After several hours they were able to account for everyone.

"Thank God there were no fatalities," said Sheriff Jones. "There are some injured people, banged up mostly. The animals are scared and running around wild. I think we will have them all caught up soon," he was telling a news reporter from Kansas City.

"It's been a way long time since we've seen dad, mom," said Molly. "Maybe we should go out and look around to see if we can find him."

They cautiously exited the building. The storm had left debris laying all around the fairground buildings and grounds, luckily enough it didn't take a direct hit. The parking lot didn't fare so well. There were vehicles piled on top of each other and strewn everywhere.

There was a car with a tree limb sticking out of the side. Another was rolled up in a ball.

"Oh my God, this is awful," said Cherry.

RJ had trotted off to go get the truck. He felt something land on his shoulder as he was running southeast away from the fairground. He turned around just in time to see a whirling cloud of dirt and debris headed straight for him.

He managed to get to the truck and start the engine, but before he could shut the door he was sucked out and watched helplessly as the truck spun out of control beneath him. He was still conscious when he found himself several hundred feet in the air getting beat senseless by the swirling debris swept up in the gigantic monster.

The last thing he remember was how much static electricity there was inside this beast. Then he blacked out from pain.

Searchers and first responders swarmed the scene. There were a few minor injuries from people still on the fairgrounds. There were a few severely injured people who had tried to make their escape in their vehicles.

As the authorities un piled the wreckage they knew of at least three people unaccounted for. RJ was among them. They eventually found two of the three deceased in a field about half a mile away. They found RJ's truck on its passenger side with the door hanging open. He was nowhere to be found. His wallet was in the glove compartment and keys were still in the truck ignition.

"Mrs. Jansen, is there anything that he might have on him that could identify him?" questioned the fire chief.

"Not that I can think of Chief," said a distraught Cherry.

"Wait mom, he had on his 'Roy Rogers' watch you gave him today for his birthday.

"Oh, thank you, yes Chief, he has on a 'Roy Rogers' wrist watch I gave him today for his birthday."

"That's it?" questioned the Chief. "Any scars or anything else?"

"Ahh...he has a small heart-shaped birthmark on the back of his neck. That's all I can think of."

"We'll keep searching Mrs. Jansen. We will let you know if we find him, or anything about him.

Dan and Martha came and picked Cherry, Molly and Kyle up from the fair. The mood was somber at best. Crying and sobbing they went back to the Lazy J to collect their thoughts and try to figure out what to do next.

"Get a search dog out here to see if we can track RJ," said the Sheriff.

They took the search dog over to the place where RJ was last supposed to be and released the dog. He ran around in circles for a few minutes and laid down on the ground whining.

"No joy with the search dog. Get that deputy out here to fly the radio-controlled plane to search for him."

The deputy flew for hours combing the county for anything that might resemble a body. He came back the next day and searched again. The county brought in a search plane loaded with infrared heat seeking gear to search. Nothing, no sign of RJ anywhere.

"My God, where on earth could he be?" sighed the Sheriff.

The next days they stayed turned to the TV news for anything that might tell them what was going on.

"Breaking News, hello ladies and gentlemen. As you know the last few days have been a story of mayhem and destruction across the Central and Eastern US. There were even tornadoes in Canada. So far, the count is at least 154 tornadoes touching down in several states, Oklahoma, Kansas, Nebraska, Texas and Arkansas. This outbreak on the plains has lasted over six days.

So far there have been at least 50 fatalities, several are unaccounted for, and over 900 injured. The cost in terms of property damage is going to reach over 2 billion dollars. Since there are still many individuals unaccounted for. Authorities have set up a central office to reach out to in case you're looking for someone.

At this time donations and all types of help are pouring in. The scene in several states is still chaotic and fluid. This historic outbreak will no doubt be documented as one of the worst of all time.

Our hearts and prayers go out to all those affected by this event. There is at the bottom of the screen phone numbers to call for information on lost loved ones and for where donations can be sent.

In other news."

"We're not alone in this situation guys. People all over the region are picking up pieces of their lives," said Sheriff Jones.

"What do we do now, Sheriff," asked Cherry.

"I don't know Cherry, for the first time in my life I'm totally flummoxed. We will keep on the lookout and praying for a successful conclusion. The Lord is our hope, Cherry.

Kyle, we will see ourselves out."

The Sheriff left and the room was struck in silence. Martha, RJ's mother, and Dan his father was absolutely stricken with fear.

"I've never seen anything like it," said Dan. "One minute everything is peaceful and the next it's a war zone. They say that's how it goes with tornadoes, calm and then destruction. I've never actually seen one in person."

"Cherry, you and the kids are welcome to stay with us for a few days until the shock wears off," said Martha. "How long has it been since you've eaten?"

"I was about to eat a corndog when a piece of cardboard smacked me in the face...I dropped the corndog in the excitement," said a frazzled Kyle.

"I guess I'm hungry too," said Molly. "I look like I've been in a tornado. What a mess, that stuff flying by stung like a bee. My skin is still raw."

The chef at the Lazy J served up some burgers and fries and topped off with a chocolate milk shake.

Cherry sat there trembling.

"I'm not sure I can keep anything down right now," she said.

"How long do you think they will keep searching?"

"They will only go on for a few days. Unless they find some evidence to support a continued search. They only have so many resources to go around as it is," said Dan.

"When you guys are done eating. Come with me to the house and we will bed you down there for tonight. You can go home tomorrow.

Oh, the fire chief called and said they found your animals. You can pick them up tomorrow. They will hold the auction next weekend after everything has settled down," said Martha.

Chapter Two

"Fruitless Search"

"I'm sorry to tell you this Mrs. Jansen. We have called off the search for RJ. We have combed the county and the counties surrounding and found nothing. If we get any new information, we'll let you know immediately. We are very sorry for your loss," said the Emergency Response director.

"What was supposed to be a day of celebration turned into the worst possible mess," said Martha.

Martha was grieving the loss of her son and the utter sadness and despair of her daughter in law and grandchildren. Douglas rushed home from medical school to be by his mother's side.

"Mom, I just can't believe he's dead. I feel somehow in my heart that he's still alive. He has to be somewhere. You can't just vanish off the face of the earth and leave no trace. Well, normally you can't!" said Douglas.

The entire Jansen family gathered for a memorial for RJ after three months of no new information.

Tom and Marsha arrived and declared that they would remain vigilant watching the news for anything that might produce a lead.

Lanora and Darren pledged any support they could. Dan and Martha were keeping Cherry, Molly and Kyle from losing it altogether.

Molly and Kyle would soon be off to university as they had indeed won those coveted scholarships. Douglas was nearing the end of his medical school training and was getting ready to go to internships.

Cherry's clinic carried on; she went in daily just to break the monotony, if nothing else. She needed to be needed by someone. The clinic provided some relief from the pain of their loss.

Dan and Martha determined to learn what had happened to their son, started making small trips to see if they could gather any information.

Mandy, seeing an opportunity, took over the reins of the Lazy J casual and fine dining restaurant. Lea, working her job at the TV station spread the news as often as she could work it in to the news cycle. She was determined to keep getting the word out.

The authorities gave up the ground and air search but continued to monitor anything that might come over the wire services.

Cherry sat on the sofa at home, curled up in a ball and sobbed quietly. She had a new Sammy to comfort her. The new Sammy was a four pound two-year-old Yorkshire Terrier. She curled up in her lap and they both watched reruns of the 'Roy Rogers' show on TV.

With her children off at school. Cherry found that she could get lonely pretty quickly. She would need to find other things to do besides sit and mourn for RJ. She started going to the library and searching for news articles that might reveal some shred of information.

In the meantime.

A stock truck and trailer had been traveling southbound on the Interstate highway. It had passed through the worst outbreak of tornadoes the Plains had seen in a hundred years. The driver pulling a load that was carrying about fifty head of sheep and was headed for a final destination of Cuernavaca, a small city south of Mexico City.

He disconnected his trailer in San Antonio Texas and headed back north for another load. The trailer was soon picked up by a different trucking company. The driver connected the trailer and headed south across the border to its final destination.

It took about three- or four-days' time to complete the rest of the journey. The driver parked the trailer at the Cuernavaca stock yards where it sat for a few hours waiting on the drovers to take the herd on out of town to a ranch where thousands of sheep were grazing.

The team opened up the trailer gate and started moving the sheep out of the trailer marking them with the ranches tags as they went by. Suddenly the sheep stopped moving, even with encouragement, they stood there.

"Hey, sheep, let's go," said one of the ranch hands.

"Weird, it looks like they are protecting something. Maybe one of them had a lamb or something on the trip down. Come on sheep, we don't have all day."

One of the hands having had enough with the frustrating situation jumped up into the trailer and started heading for the cluster of sheep. The sheep gathered even closer together and began baying loudly.

"What in the devil has got into you crazy animals?"

He approached carefully and had to drag the animals away from whatever they were protecting. One by one he got them to move out of the way.

"Oh my God. Come up here, now Pedro. You've got to see this for yourself."

Pedro climbed into the trailer. What, he thought to himself, could be so interesting.

He jumped back, "What the heck," he demanded.

Between them they were able to get the remaining sheep down the ramp. Revealing a body of a man lying on his side, unconscious with a sharp stick protruding out of his right shoulder and a visible depression on the side of his skull.

"Oh my, call an ambulance, I think he's breathing. How did he get in here?"

The ambulance roared up, paramedics jumped out and assessed the bodies condition.

"He's pretty beat up," said one paramedic. "We need to get him to the nearest hospital quickly."

The workers were left with a million questions.

"Who was that guy?" asked the foreman for the ranch. "Did he get beat up by a cartel and thrown in the trailer to get rid of him? Where did he come from? I wonder if he will live? The side of his head was bashed in pretty good. If he's alive he lucky to be, when he wakes up, he might think different. That has got to hurt."

Chapter Three

"The Man who Fell from the SKY"

The ambulance sirens and lights blazing ran the few miles to the nearest hospital that could take care of such an injured person.

They pulled into the emergency room awning and unloaded the man and brought him into the bay. The nurses and doctor on duty surrounded him and asked their usual questions, vital signs, where did he come from, who is he?

The paramedics told them where he was found and that he had no identifying information on him. The only thing he had on him was a t-shirt, blue jeans, work boots, a plain wedding ring and a wrist watch with a cowboy's face on it, and the words, 'Roy Rogers.'

"Well, I guess for the time being until we know otherwise, he will be Roy Rogers," said the Doctor in charge.

"Let's get him cleaned up and run through the CT scan and Xray machines. Get him prepped for surgery to get that piece of wood out of his shoulder."

The hospital staff complied and got the immediate issues handled. He was dehydrated severely, the wound on his shoulder was infected so they got an anti-biotic going. The CT scan showed several broken ribs and fractured vertebrae in the spine, his shoulders were dislocated and his left hip was dislocated, there was lots of soft tissue that was damaged, some of it likely beyond repair. Several muscles on the outside of his left hip were torn completely through.

"His skull is damaged with a deep visible depression on the left side," said the technician.

"Ok, call in the neurosurgeon. He's going to need a spinal fusion immediately. He will need his skull repaired as well. In the location of the depression, he might or might not have any memory or at least limited memory when and if he wakes up.

"He will eventually need a hip replacement on the left side, but it can wait," said the attending, Doctor.

The neurosurgeon operated to relieve the pressure on the man's skull. They took a break and brought in a whole new team and performed a four-level 360-degree fusion on his lower spine.

"Well Roy Rogers, or whomever you are. If and when you wake up, I have a few questions of my own," said the head, Doctor.

"Where did you say he came from?" asked the hospital administrator.

"He was found in the back of a stock trailer, unconscious and in urgent need of medical care," said one of the paramedics that brought him into the hospital.

"I know that, where did he come from?" I asked.

"The current theory is that he fell from the sky. Or got mugged by the cartel and tossed into the trailer to dispose of the evidence. Don't ask me how or when. The man had been in the bed of the trailer for at least five days or maybe even longer. They say the trailer had traveled from as far away as Wisconsin in the US and traveled through a swarm of tornadoes while traveling south to San Antonio.

Strangely enough, he could have very well have been swept up in one of those storms and deposited in the back of the trailer. Fortunately for him, it was a soft landing, into a moving target."

"What do you mean, soft landing," asked the administer.

"He landed in a truck full of sheep," chuckled the paramedic.

"If he's not dead in forty-eight hours I need to find someone to care for him," said the administrator. "Is there really nothing to identify him? I need to send the bill for all this to somebody."

The man lapsed into a coma. After two weeks in intensive care the staff felt he was stable enough to be transferred to a long-term care facility. Off they sent him to Sunny Acres assistive living center. Him, and all his hoses and wires took up residence in a ward with windows facing to the south. Light would shine in on him daily, as the sun moved east to west.

Roy Rogers developed some new friends at Sunny Acres. He had some ward mates that would talk to him and read to him daily. The attendants felt kindly towards him, wondering who he might have left behind in his unlikely travels.

"I think he has a wife and many children," said Maria one of the staff attendants.

"I think he was a rodeo cowboy," said another.

Still others speculated and wondered who the mystery man was and where he came from, falling out the sky as he did.

Roy Rogers was in fact getting healthier day by day.

No one in the US knew about 'Sky Man' or Roy Rogers, and he was a delightful mystery in Mexico sparking many conspiracies and theories.

At home in Pine Creek, everyone thought maybe he had just been covered over by debris and expired. Even still those closest to RJ felt in their hearts that he was somewhere, alive. Maybe he just can't get back to them yet.

Cherry searched on and on. Friends would come and help her sometimes, even they finally gave up. Nobody knew what they were looking for.

Roy had some doting young attendants in the Sunny Acres home. They kept him fed, shaved, bathed and all, they helped him carry out all the necessities of life. Even they began to dwindle over time.

He had one remaining young attendant, a young girl named Lolita, she talked to him and read to him occasionally. She would squeeze his hand every now and then, just to see if anything would happen.

It was going on seven months since he was admitted to Sunny Acres. Sunny Acres was needing bed space and was wishing he would die or wake up. Lolita prayed a new prayer for Sky Man.

"Lord, please help Mr. Roy wake up and be healthy."

On the beginning of the eighth month, Lolita squeezed his hand, and he squeezed her hand back. She nearly fainted. She looked up at his face and his eyes were following her every move.

Lolita ran down the hallway screaming at the top of her lungs. "Sky Man is awake; Sky Man is awake."

People came running from all over the center to see if it was true. It was, in fact, true.

He sat up in the bed and said, "I'm hungry, can I get a steak?"

Lolita squealed with joy. Her prayers had been answered. Wait until everyone at home hears about this.

The Doctor came over and checked him out from top to bottom.

"Tell us Sky Man, who are you and where did you fall from?" said the Doctor.

"Maybe you know yourself better as 'Roy Rogers,' that's the name on your wrist watch. It has an inscription on the back that says, "Roy...HBD...CJ."

Roy looked at the crowed room and searched for words.

"I have no idea who I am or where I came from. The last thing I remember was floating in the sky, suddenly I blacked out, and then you showed up. Who are you and where am I now?" he puzzled.

The head nurse spoke up first. "You are in southern Mexico in a convalescent facility. You've been here for nearly eight months. You had a very bad bump on the head, the doctors said you might not have much memory left. You also had a spinal fusion to correct many twisted and broken vertebrae. Your left side has sustained heavy damage to soft tissue. Many of your muscles are now detached and are inoperable. You will need a hip replacement sometime soon. Yes, I think that might be about all. How do you feel Mr. Roy?"

"I don't know. My head hurts a bit. My side is stiff and painful. My back feels pretty solid. I'm not sure what to say, I will know more when I attempt to walk."

"We will get you into physical therapy as soon as tomorrow Mr. Roy. As far as the steak is concerned, we will bring your diet along very slowly. We don't want to overfeed you too quickly. You've had a very difficult experience Mr. Roy. It will take time to get you moving again. Fortunately for you, you seemed to be in otherwise good physical shape, besides the obvious. You will certainly have stories to tell someday. Are you married; do you have children?"

Once again Roy... or if you must, SKY Man... looked dazed and confused.

I have no idea, judging by the ring on my left hand. I am or was. Maybe they are searching for me?"

"There is no way to tell, Mr. Roy. We've had no outside contacts or inquires looking for Roy Rogers."

RJ's rehab began slowly the next day. His legs were like jelly and everything hurt. He worked at it vigorously. He needed to find home. He must get his legs back so he can find home.

In the third month after starting rehabilitation, he was able to walk with a cane and get around fairly well. He was doing well physically, but he was getting board. Lolita was a big help. She had also helped him with his Spanish. They went on walks and she talked him through the various phrases he would need to communicate effectively.

"What do you want to do next?" Lolita asked him.

"I want to find my home and my family," he told her. "As soon as I am able, I will begin the search for my home."

He started nosing around for something to do and found some old pieces of a satellite dish in a shed. Pretty soon he had built a working satellite system for the Sunny Acres residents to enjoy TV.

"Oh my, Mr. Roy. What have you done?" asked the head nurse. "We can now get 247 channels. Everyone is glued to their favorite football teams games. This is the greatest thing to happen here in like ... forever."

Roy continued finding things to fix. Broken TVs, radios, beds, light fixtures, he even helped install a new computer in the office. Soon he had a new name, Mr. Fix it.

One day Roy woke up and couldn't find anything to fix. He wandered into town and found the local police department. He asked them if they needed anything fixed. Before long Roy, Mr. Fix it, had set up a little shop in a side building beside the police department office. He would wander back to Sunny Acres to eat and sleep.

Then one day he wandered in to a local shop and asked if they needed anything fixed?

"No Senor, but I can help you with your search. I will get you an ID and Passport so you can travel in search of your home."

Roy gladly accepted his new credentials, it said, Roy Rogers, and gave Sunny Acres as his home address.

"Thank you, kind sir," spoke Roy. "I will keep them very safe. I must begin my search for home."

He turned around, went out the door, and off he wandered. With what little money he had been able to collect from fixing things, he caught a bus to the eastern coast of Mexico. No one in the town of Cuernavaca or Sunny Acres every saw or heard of him again.

One year had passed by this time. Everyone at home was trying to forget about the tornadic experience of May 1999. There were many theories as to what might have happened to RJ. Cherry never gave up hope and enlisted her sister-in-law Marsha to help comb this new-fangled thing called the Internet.

"Cherry you still need to eat, come over to the restaurant for a hot meal, please," said Martha.

"Ok, I'm just finishing up a search of Canada, I'll be right there."

"Have you found anything, anything at all." quizzed Martha.

"No, nothing, but there is still a mountain range of places to look. I know I will find something."

"Dan is in contact with his former colleagues, they haven't found anything either."

"I have found one thing," said Cherry. "That darn Insurance man is bugging me to death to have RJ declared dead so he can finish his paperwork. I'm about to lose it with him. I told him, no body, no insurance, get over it. He says I have three years to wrap this up myself or the government will do it for me. Ugg, just leave me alone I told him."

"I've polled all my old contacts in the FBI," said Marsha. "They haven't heard or seen anything that might be a clue. Has Dan heard anything from his contacts?"

"No, and he's getting despondent about it," said Martha.

"How are the kids doing at school? It's their first year and away from home," asked Marsha.

"They are both hurting, Molly calls one day and Kyle the next. They are doing what they are doing with school because they know that's what dad would want them to do. They say time heals all wounds. I'm not sure about that. Every time someone asks me about Roy it's like I just found out about it and I'm a complete mess all over again. Sometimes I just want to hide. I know people are curious and mean well. If we just had any news, any news at all," said Cherry.

Chapter Four

"SKY MAN follows his nose"

Somehow Roy got his sense of direction messed up and began his search for home by heading east to the Caribbean coast and then eventually to the south. He found his way to Cancun and wandered into a resort hotel and asked if they needed anything fixed?

The person at the front desk looked at him and recognized him from a newspaper article published in the towns paper about 'Sky Man' on the move. Beware it says, he wants to fix everything, so keep an eye out and your TVs antenna at a safe distance. The article was a few weeks old and was jokingly of course.

The resort happily employed Roy with multitudes of articles that needed fixing. There had been a hurricane come through recently and the pile of broken stuff was filling a storage room to the brim. They gave him food and shelter and soon enjoyed watching 247 channels on their newly installed satellite dish.

"Hey boss look at this." The deputy was referring to the Sheriff of Pine Creek. I've been videotaping the Carson show for several weeks now, while I'm at work. I like to watch it when I get up in the afternoon.

He does these strange story segments in his monologue; he hatched a new one a few weeks ago. These tapes are several weeks old and the monologue is pretty out dated as well. I'm just now starting to catch up.

They watched the video as Carson comes on with his monologue for that particular night.

"So, ladies and gentlemen, you too Ed, and over there is Doc and his merry band of minstrels. So strange story of the week. Here is an interesting one out of southern Mexico. My team has been following this story for some time now. We decided it might be news worthy so here we go.

A man, who has now garnered the moniker of 'Sky Man' was found in the bed of an 18-wheeler that was hauling a load of sheep. He was found badly beaten and unconscious but alive. They had no idea who he was or where he came from. They patched him up and put him in a ward with all the usual hoses, cables and such attached to him and pretty much left him there.

He laid there in a coma for nearly eight months' time, and then suddenly, he awakened. They had also discovered that he had a 'Roy Rogers' wrist watch on him. When he first became aware of his surroundings, he had no idea who he was or where he was from. Since the man had sustained a pretty substantial skull fracture the doctors were not surprised by his memory situation.

Heck, Ed, I wake everyday with memory problems, who is that over there holding that trumpet?"

Audience laughter.

"Anyway, the guy goes through some physical therapy and next thing you know he's fixing anything he can find around the hospital. They transferred him to a long-term care facility to finish rehab.

Before they knew it, they had a new satellite dish on the roof and it was picking up 247 channels.

"What," says Ed, I'm lucky if I can pick up four channels and that's if the rabbit ears are pointed in the right direction."

Audience laughter.

"So, Sky Man, before he suddenly up and left on his search for his home, acquired a new name, 'Roy Rogers,' since that was the only thing on him that could identify him. Roy Rogers stuck.

Hey Roy, if you're out there listening, my TV is busted and I can't get anyone to come and fix the thing. If you happen to wander up north, I've got a job for you buddy.

And that my friends are the strange story of the week. Apparently, Sky Man or Roy Rogers is on the move. We will keep an eye out for any updates.

What do you think Doc, where is this guy from?"

"I think he's from Kansas, isn't that were the land of OZ is, I hear they have rainbows up there sometimes too. Who knows, he might have got his training under 'The Wizard.'"

Audience laughter.

"Sheriff what do you think? Could this be the missing Mr. Jansen?"

"Let's see more of those tapes Deputy."

"Ok, this one is about a month old, Carson says that Sky Man has moved to Cancun and checked into a resort."

Carson talking. "Hey Ed, Doc, remember that guy Sky Man or Roy Rogers?"

"Yeah, what's he doing now?" says Ed.

"He checked into a resort in Cancun and well, he didn't really check in. He went there looking for any sign of his home and found a welcoming committee instead, and a pile of stuff to fix. Telephones, TVs, Radios, electrical boxes, you name it. They gave him a bed and food in return for his work. He stayed there for a couple of weeks and with a bit of money he made there he caught a bus. We'll have to keep watching the news to see where he wound up."

"Did the resort get a satellite dish too?" laughed Doc.

"Yep, sure did, he's getting the entire Caribbean and southern Mexico hooked up with 247 channels. I'm getting more jealous by the day."

Audience laughter.

"Ok folks, we will keep you informed. As we get more news."

"Sheriff...what do you think?"

"Can I have those tapes? Or a copy of them?"

"Sure, I'll have them copied for you this afternoon." said the deputy.

The phone rang at the Jansen residence. Douglas picked up the receiver.

"Cherry this is Sheriff Jones."

"Sheriff, this is Douglas, can I help you?"

"Oh good, Douglas, I have something you need to see. I don't want to alarm your mother or get her hopes up but, we might have found something regarding RJ's whereabouts."

"You're kidding?"

"No, not kidding. Can I drop the tapes by this evening?"

"Sure, thing Sheriff. See you then."

Douglas found Cherry at her usual spot scanning the internet for any information that might lead them to Roy.

"Mom, Sheriff Jones says they might have found something and he wants to drop it by this evening for you to see. Apparently, it's some old videotapes."

"Of course, Douglas, let him in when he gets here."

"Mom, could you please get away from that thing for a while. We need to visit about other things going on in our lives, mom!"

"Yes dear, I'll just be a minute more."

"Ok mom, a minute was up an hour ago."

"Ok dear, what's on your mind?"

"I'm asking my girlfriend Nancy to marry me. We want to have the wedding at the church in June. What do you think?"

"Ah...Nancy, wedding in June, is she the blond or the brunette? OH, MY Douglas where have I been these last months?"

"Mom, she's the redhead. It's pretty obvious mom, you've been searching for dad on the internet. Come back to earth for a few minutes. My residency is done and I'm going to take a position in a hospital in Kansas City as an Orthopedic Surgeon. I'll be living fairly close to Uncle Tom and Aunt Marsha. They will be a great help getting settled."

"Oh dear, that's so great. I'm absolutely thrilled for you. Remind me again, who's Nancy? Just kidding dear."

The doorbell rang, Douglas rushed over to greet Sheriff Jones. New Sammy announced his arrival as well. She stood there panting while he came into the room with an arm load of VHS tapes.

"What's all this, Sheriff?" asked Cherry.

"Well, we think we might have discovered a link to the whereabouts of RJ. You will need to see these tapes from the Carson Show."

"What, the Carson Show. I haven't watched the TV in years," said Cherry.

"Put one on," said Douglas.

The Sheriff slid one of the tapes into the slot of the recorder, grabbed the remote and started it up. The machine clicked and started up with a bit of a moan.

"Haven't used it in a while eh," said the Sheriff.

He played the first two episodes. Cherry and Douglas stood there wide eyed.

"Is there more?" she blurted out.

"Yes, a lot more, keep watching, we're just beginning."

"Hey ladies and Gentlemen, it's time for our weekly roundup of strange news. So, we've been following the exploits of Sky Man out of Mexico, he's now better known as 'Roy Rogers.'

According to some news reports that have just come in, Roy left the shelter of the resort at Cancun and took a bus farther south and found a small ranch where he introduced himself and asked if there were things he could fix in exchange for a bed and some food?

The rancher had never heard of Sky Man and or Roy Rogers and ran him off the property. He soon found himself on the edge of a small town and was greeted by a gang of thieves. The ruffians had the local business people terrified and were taking money from them regularly.

Roy approached them and they started to harass him. He shrugged it off until they started at him with ball bats. The reports say, he snatched one of the ball bats away and did a thorough beat down of the thugs, much to the delight of the local crowd.

It appears Roy Rogers may have some military background, ED."

"I would say so, Jonny. He can handle himself. His legend grows day by day."

"What do you think Doc?"

"Well, you can guarantee the Wizard didn't teach him any of that handiwork," said Doc.

Audience laughter.

"Hey I'm waiting for the TV series to come out. This guy isn't just a Mr. fix it of stuff. I can see it now, 'The Legend of Sky Man' on the small screen. Hey I wonder who could be the lead? I'm thinking Clint might be a good one. He does lots of traveling westerns," said Jonny.

"Nah, I think Harrison would be better. You know the rugged, think on your feet kinda guy," said Ed.

"One way or the other this guy is getting a lot of attention. Curiosity is being generated all over with people guessing who he might be. Until next week ladies and gentlemen."

"Can we see one or two more," asked Cherry.

"Sure, said the Sheriff, I think there are only two more of these anyway. The show has gone into reruns so this is it for a while."

"Who's up for this week's update on the Sky Man saga," asked Jonny.

The audience goes wild. Loud applause.

"That's what I thought, said Jonny. Ed, can you guess what's up next with the Sky Man?"

"All I know is 247 channels is my dream, any chance we could track this guy down and hire him?"

"Good question, Doc, you want to hazard a guess?"

"Let's see," says Doc, "if I'm a betting man I'd say he stumbled into something lucrative and is living the life of Riley."

"Well, you're both wrong. But first I think we might have caught a break; control says they think they have found a video of the guy strolling through the countryside. Roll the tape control."

Tape rolls, the audience gasps. Then roars with laughter and applause.

"Oh man, that's not Sky Man, that's the bigfoot video. Sorry folks we will search and see if we can find the right video. Ah yes, control says this is the right one. Roll the tape control."

Tape rolls, the audience sits there silent.

"Hum, that's a mugshot from a prison in Venezuela. I hope that's not him. Kinda fuzzy anyway. Well until next week. Oh wait, Doc says he has a new theme song for this segment."

Doc and the orchestra play a few strains of "Happy Trails to You."

"Well, that was stupid," said Douglas.

"They're getting a lot of mileage out of this situation, it's a ratings bonanza for them," said the Sheriff. "There is one more on this tape."

Jonny taps his cards on the desk and takes a drink of whatever is in his cup on the desk.

"Ladies and gentlemen, we have some breaking news with the Sky Man saga. He has either fallen off the edge of the earth, jumped on a Cruise ship, or been kidnapped by a tramp steamer ship's crew and pressed into service. Either way, we can't find any new evidence of him anywhere. We do have a couple of rumors we are following up on."

"That sounds pretty ominous," says Doc. So... 247 channels are out of the question for now?"

"Looks like that's it for now Doc, Ed is over here sobbing in his handkerchief. Until next season folks, we're saying, Happy Trails Roy, hope you find your way home soon. If you do give us a call, we'd love to have you on the show."

"Bummer," said Douglas.

"These tapes are weeks old and the information on them was months old. Maybe Dan can get with some of his contacts to see if he can find out where they were getting their information.

Chapter Five

"Chasing the Truth"

Dan started checking with his contacts on the east coast. In the meantime, with some sense of direction the Jansen family internet search ground on. They managed to find some actual articles published months ago from the south of Mexico and points south about a man that fell from the sky and went around helping people while he searched for his home.

Those articles ended months ago with nothing further reported. In fact, the wandering do-gooder actually provoked a stream of imposters that were taking advantage of people. They would pretend to be 'Roy Rogers' and make an agreement to work and then rip them off.

As far as Mexico and central America were concerned 'Sky Man,' aka 'Roy Rogers,' was a bandit. No one wanted anything to do with him anymore.

Dan traveled out to Los Angeles and managed to work his way into the studios where the Carson show was produced and scheduled a meet with one of the producers.

"Yes sir, can I help you?" said the assistant.

"I'm here to see Ms. Carpenter."

"Wait here, she will be out in a minute."

"Hello I'm Ms. Carpenter, how can I help you?"

"Can we go somewhere private to visit for a minute?"

"Certainly, follow me."

They went into her office. She sat down at a cluttered desk with articles and notes stuck everywhere.

"Have a seat, er, ah, Mr. Jansen, is it?"

"Yes, it is. Thank you for seeing me. Let me begin by saying we really enjoy the show. With that out of the way. I have a question concerning the series of episodes where Jonny, Ed and Doc are talking about this fellow that dropped out of the sky. I believe they have dubbed him 'Sky Man' or 'Roy Rogers.'

My question is where did they come by this information?"

"Well sir, our sources are confidential. You understand that I'm bound by a Non-Disclosure Agreement to keep those types of information under wraps. There is little I can tell you."

"Ms. Carpenter, I have reason to believe that the person you have been monologuing about is my missing son. He may have been swept up in a large tornado in the Midwest in May of 1999 and hasn't been seen or heard of since, until your broadcast began the series of stories about a man falling from the sky."

"I see Mr. Jansen. Well, since that series began our ratings have skyrocketed, if you will mind the pun. The show runners are not likely to give it up easily. Let me make a quick phone call, please wait outside."

"I will be happy to. Any shred of information could be very valuable in finding our son. Please help."

"Hello, yeah, I have this guy in my office that says the sky man / Roy Rogers might be his missing son. He's looking for any information on his life and location. What do you want me to tell him? Yes, I know it's mostly made up. We took a snippet out of a newspaper article and created an entire back story. Ok, I will give him one bit and send him on. Yes, I know, sky man is killing it for us. Ok, bye."

"Mr. Jansen, in lieu of the situation and us protecting our sources and our future ratings I can give you one thing only. It is the only truth I have and the only one you will get from our company."

"Ok, I'll take whatever I can get, thank you Ms. Carpenter."

"Wait outside. I'll be with you in a moment."

Dan sat outside and tapped his fingers on the chair arm rests. After about ten minutes the assistant emerged with an envelope and handed it to him.

"Please take this and do not open it here. Wait until you're back in your hotel or where ever to open it and you didn't get it from here, understand!"

"Yes, I understand."

Dan left the studio and went back to the hotel and opened the envelope. Inside was a very brief article from a Mexican newspaper describing the unusual event. There was a note attached. Everything after the publication of this article is pure showmanship, full stop. Best of Luck.

Dans' demeanor lifted and then sunk to depths he had never experienced before. On one hand the smallest bit of information is helpful. Then again, RJ could be just about anywhere by now. Not knowing if he was alive or dead didn't help either. It was clear the TV show was going to run with the thread as long as it produced results. Time to go home.

"Martha, this is Dan, I'm on my way home. I'll see you in the morning. I have to check something out first and then I'll catch the first available plane home."

"Ok Dan, anything worth reporting?"

"No, it was a dead end. Actually, it was worse than a dead end. See you tomorrow."

Dan called up one of his old contacts.

"Hey, have your guys heard anything of an American wandering around Mexico or Central America with no idea where he's from or his real name?"

"Ah...Dan...there's a bunch of Americans wandering around down there with their brains fried on drugs. People come down there on vacation and wind up in a ditch or worse in a psych ward loony as a duck. We try to locate and repatriate as many as we can. There are lots of people that make it down and back home just fine, but there are quite a few that don't. What makes this one different?

"Well, we believe our son RJ, Roy Jansen was caught up in a tornado and dumped into the bed of an 18-wheeler full of sheep and ended up in south Mexico with amnesia and a host of internal and external injuries. We believe he was treated at a hospital in Cuernavaca Mexico and then transferred to a long-term care facility while in coma. There's no more reliable information after that.

Have you heard anything or seen anything on the wires?"

"Huh...you're talking about the guy that ended up with the moniker, 'SKY MAN,' or Roy Rogers, aren't you?"

"Yes, that's him, have you got anything?"

"Yeah, only information is that he better not show his face or let his self out in the open. Authorities all over down there are looking for him. The imposters have flooded the area and are taking advantage of his story to rip people off. If he's smart, he's under cover and staying very low. I will say this, he may have someone helping him. We've had some rumors that popped up and might be worth checking out. Our guys are really busy with more important issues Dan. I will send out an alert for them to be on the lookout for him. How would they know he's the real deal Dan?"

"He has a small birthmark on the left side back of his neck that looks like a small heart. He also wears a special wrist watch his wife gave him for his birthday recently. It's a commemorative 'Roy Rogers' wrist watch. It has an inscription on the back. Roy...HBD...CJ."

"Ok Dan, anything else that might help us?"

"Not that I can think of. Wait a minute. He might be trying to get to Panama. He spent a good deal of time down there in the Airforce at Howard AFB. He might be remembering those surroundings and believes that's home. He stayed in the Canal Zone for quite a while, it's just a guess, but who knows. Let me know if you hear of anything, please. Dan out."

Dan dropped his suitcase at the door of his and Martha's home. He went to the back of the house and sat on the edge of the bed and sobbed.

Martha came in and sat beside him and held him tightly.

He struggled to speak.

"Where is our boy Martha, where is he?"

"Did they give you any information at all?"

"Yes, the whole this is based on one snippet of an article and the rest of it is all made up. If they did know something else, they were not about to share. I'm exhausted, I need to talk to Cherry, but I can't do it right now."

Cherry sat in front of her bedroom mirror. She looked at herself and watched as her face melted away, leaving only the outside edges. Her soft flowing beautiful white hair was turning a bland lifeless shade of pale.

She whispered at the self in the mirror. "I must let go. I don't know how. I feel helpless and paralyzed."

She reached out to touch the mirror. The image faded to gray. She had passed out, her head lying on the dresser table.

She didn't know how long she was out. While she was out, she dreamed she saw RJ in a tropical setting, looking for home he said, he was asking everyone he came to if they knew where his home was.

Suddenly she sat straight up and blurted out. "He has amnesia and doesn't know where he is. I know it, I can feel it. He's alive and searching." Just then she heard a still small voice in her ear, it said, "Take heart my child, the wind still blows, and the sun rises again."

What, was that, she thought, either way I need to get up and get moving. My heart is filled with a new hope. I must believe and trust that we will connect again.

Cherry cleaned up, got dressed and drove herself over to the Lazy J restaurant. She went in and sat down. Soon the server came over and addressed her.

"Good day Dr. Jansen. How may I help you?"

"I need a coffee and some apple pie. Please."

"Coming right up ma'am."

She picked up the new hand-held device that Douglas bought her recently. She looked at the keyboard on the thing and dialed Martha's phone number.

"Hello, Martha speaking."

"Hello Martha this is Cherry. I'm over at the Lazy J. Have you the time to come and join me?"

"Sure honey, I'll be over in a few minutes."

The bell rang over the door and Martha smiled at her when she entered the room.

"What's going on Cherry, I haven't seen you so shiny in a while?"

"I finally hit that bottom you hear so much about, a voice at the bottom told me to get up and get moving, things are going to get better. While I was unconscious, I had a vision of Roy trapsing around a tropical setting asking everyone he came to if this was his home. I'm convinced Martha, he's alive and wandering around somewhere way south of here. Now that I know what to pray for, I'll be earnestly seeking God's will for Roy to regain his memory and find his path to home."

"I don't know what to say dear. I think you might be on to something. I will join you right now. Lord, please help us, we praise you and believe and trust you that Roy Jansen regains his memory and finds his way home. By the Holy Spirit we pray in Jesus' name, make it so."

"Amen Martha. I'm going to go back to work tomorrow and I also have a wedding to get ready for. The truth is rising to the surface Martha, God's most excellent will, will prevail.

I need some more of that Apple Pie."

"Come to think of it, I could use a slice myself. I might grab an extra slice and go cheer up Dan. He's having a rough time of it also. Apple Pie will help. It always did before."

Days and weeks passed with no word. Something told her to watch the Carson show that night. She decided to video tape it just for fun.

"Hey there folks, and all of you fans in the studio audience. You're looking mighty fit today, what is this yoga stretch day or something."

Audience laughter.

"I mean really, I haven't seen some much spandex since the Senior Prom, you know the one they hold down at the Sunny Palms Senior Center."

Audience laughter.

"So, Ed, Doc, you remember that guy Roy Rogers or Sky Man we used to call him. He's been on the move again."

"How do you know Jonny?" asked Doc.

"There is a trail of satellite dishes all along the coast of Belize, Honduras, Nicaragua, Costa Rica, and now he's been sighted in Panama, he was sighted up on the roof of the local hospital hooking up a new satellite dish."

Ed groans, "Oh man, when is he coming back north? My TV set is all snow and scratchy since the El Nino blew down my antenna."

Doc chuckles, "I'd loan you mine but the lighting took it out, last week. So much for sunny California."

"Anyway, they had to get him down off the roof, a group of policemen mistook him for a bandit and were taking pot shots at him. He waved at the crowd and then they had to call in crowd control when they recognized him. People lined up for miles to get a glimpse of SKY MAN. They really wanted one of those dishes, apparently 247 channels are very popular down there."

"So, what happened next," asked Ed.

"A band of traveling gypsies in a circus bus snagged him and drove off into the jungle."

"What," shrieked Doc. Is he gone forever?"

"Maybe the natives want 247 channels as well. You know I've seen those dishes hanging from the side of Palm Trees. He had better be careful, he might fall on his head again and turn north and install satellite dishes all up the west coast."

"Well, that wouldn't be such a bad thing," said Ed.

Audience laughter.

"Oops, another update just came in. Roy Rogers was seen boarding a RORO ship in the Canal Zone carrying a satellite dish under each arm. What on earth is he up to now."

Audience laughter.

"Ed's still over there sobbing into his handkerchief, Ed, get a hold of yourself MAN."

The audience roars with laughter.

Doc's orchestra breaks out in a rendition of 'Happy Trails to you.'

Cherry sat there for a minute stunned. She grabbed the video tape out of the machine and called Dan.

"I'm sorry, I know it's late. I need you to see something."

She drove over to Dan and Martha's house and banged on the door.

"What is it honey?" questioned a sleepy-eyed Martha. "Dan will be in in a minute."

"I videotaped the Carson show tonight. I want Dan to watch it and see if he gets the same thing I got."

Dan comes in finishing tying his robe together and grabs his glasses.

"What have you got here young lady?" said Dan.

"This is tonight's episode of the Carson show, I taped it just for fun. Watch and see if you get out of it what I think I got."

They plugged in the tape and the TV spang to life. Carson and crew go through the monologue.

"Well, it was kinda funny. My gut impression Cherry. Somebody is sending coded messages to somebody using Carsons' monologue. There must be a lot of somebodies that need to get a message out far and wide. Brilliant actually. No dead drops to deal with, no encrypted emails, no snail mail, no scrambled voice phone calls. Out in the open on TV no less."

"What are they saying and who are they saying it too?"

"My guess is, it's the State Department talking to all their stations and maybe the CIA. What I got out of it was that RJ is alive and doing some kind of work for some agency or another and is currently in and around Panama. Only the target audience would know for sure. Does it explain anything to us? Maybe, sort of. It does make me incredibly curious. I might have to go ring some bells and see if I can find out. I might start with Ballard. He could know something, then again, he's not likely to share."

"Go home Cherry, get some sleep, there might be some hope in that message or there might not. Pray on it and try to remain calm. Nothing is going to change in the near future."

"Ok Dan, good night."

Cherry left and went home. She sat in her recliner for a few minutes, Sammy jumped up and curled up in her lap. She fell asleep and dreamed the strangest dreams that night.

"Well Martha, it seems our boy is alive, the agency is using him for something."

Martha hugged Dan.

"I knew in my heart that he was alive, I just knew it.

Chapter Five

"The Jansen Children's Journey"

The van drove up to the ranch house in southwest Texas.

"This is Ballard's ranch," said the driver. "The head of Veterinary services will be out to greet you momentarily. Her name is Gretchen, her assistant's name is Ralph. They are an institution here. Mind your manners here guys, they will take good care of you."

"Thanks," said Kyle.

"Me too," said Molly.

Ballard came out and greeted them first.

"Welcome guys, let me look at you. Yep, Molly you are the spitting image of you mother, right down to that gorgeous white hair. You, Mr. Kyle, are the spitting image of your dad. I swear I'm looking at the pair of them from twenty-five years ago.

Speaking of your dad, has there been any word?"

"Nah," said Kyle. "He's the biggest mystery right now, but that's all out of our control. He would have wanted us to keep up with our lives. So here we are. We're glad you were able to let us come here and learn from your experts. This is our sophomore summer break. Next year we must declare majors. So far, we've practiced on rabbits and frogs. We need some experience with large animals to see if we want to keep going that direction."

"We are grateful Mr. Ballard," said Molly. "I understand you worked with dad back in the Vietnam war. He doesn't talk about it much, maybe you can fill us in a little bit sometime. Where do we bunk?"

"You will have private rooms in the main house. The bunk house is a pretty raw place for newcomers and no place for young ladies. You will get plenty of chances to mix with the crew. For now, you will get acclimated a little at a time. I'm not much of a believer in the old throw em in the deep end kind of training. Daily exposure to this life is going to be difficult enough.

Mark my words kids, this is way different than making show ponies shiny. This is real life on the range. We make a living by raising food for other people. Believe me, they like their food very high quality. So that's our daily goal and our moto. 'Get it right so the future is bright.' Make sense?

Here's Gretchen and Ralph, they will start working with you tomorrow on basic food quality formulas for the calves and lambs.

Gretchen and Ralph, this is Molly and Kyle Jansen. I've spoken about their father several times. They are here to learn and see if they want to do large animal veterinary work. A brief resume, their mother is a renowned children's physician and cancer researcher. She owns and operates a clinic and is a partner in their town's hospital. She met Roy Jansen, her husband and the kids' father while she was in nursing school.

They have an older brother Douglas. He's a practicing Orthopedic surgeon in Kansas City. Their father was a highly decorated noncommissioned officer the rank of Chief Master in the US Airforce. His work was mostly classified but I can tell you he was what we called a FAC or forward air controller or combat controller. You can look that up when you get the time.

Your mom and dad met at a fast-food restaurant in Sparksdale and fell madly in love, with each other, not the fast food.

Gretchen and Ralph have been employed here at Ballard Ranch for about twenty years. They know the ropes and the ins and outs of dealing with big and sometimes, small critters. You will find at least two JRT's, that's Jack Russel pups following them around where ever they go. Those pups are from a litter of Pipers. Piper and RJ, have history.

Did you know RJ started the Pop Country band named the Snake Skin Rangers? He was a self-taught guitar player and built a tour group with the idea of searching the country for Cherry. She will have to tell you about that adventure someday.

You have anything else to say, Gretchen...Ralph?"

"Just be up and ready to go early kids, five o'clock A.M. is when breakfast starts cooking. We eat a really good breakfast of high protein and carbs, because it's going to be a long day. We will take lunch about one o'clock in the afternoon. That's just about the time the sun is at its highest and when we will take a break from the heat. Do what you have to do to be up and around. Don't make anyone have to come and find you. If we have to do that, we will assume you are either deathly ill or already dead, in which case we will be calling the ambulance to come get you. Don't make me do that, it's embarrassing.

Other than that, welcome to the Ballard Ranch where we, 'Get it Right so the Future is Bright.'"

"Ralph, you got anything," said Ballard.

"Can you guys shoot? There may be times when you need to protect yourself and or the stock from predators. Can you shoot?"

"Yes sir," echoed the twins. "Dad and mom used to take us out hunting and fishing. They taught us about conservation and such, starting at a young age.

"Good, we don't want no green horn getting trussed up by an Elk or Coyote or Wolf or Bandit. Grrrrr."

They all laughed.

"Seriously...I mean it."

"Ok, Ralph, I think they get it," said Ballard.

"Look it's about dinner time, let's get some grub, what da ya say?"

"Sounds good to me," said Molly. I'm starving and I can hear Kyles stomach growling from across the room."

"Good, let's get to it."

The cook put on a fabulous meal of brisket, fried potatoes, and an onion, tomato and cucumber salad. The only noise for a few minutes was the sound of chewing, swallowing and drinking ice tea.

"Wow, that was fantastic," said Kyle.

Molly was still licking the barbecue sauce off her fingers. She mumbled something unintelligible but resembled, "me too."

They sat in the great room for a few minutes. Molly curiously got up and started walking around the room looking at all the pictures on the walls.

"These are some beautiful animals," she said.

"Who are those guys in the uniform next to you?" she asked.

Ballard got up from his chair and came over to take a look. He raised his eye glasses to get a closer look.

"Huh, well that guy on the right is your dad, he was all of twenty in that picture, next to him was his Army fellow FAC Wallace, he died in a rocket attack at Cam Rahn Bay Air Base. The guy next to him is First Lieutenant Gary Baker he was the pilot on the mission where he and your father were shot down in Panama. Next to him is me. I was the Army Airforce liaison for the FACs. I was also RJ's mentor for several missions. I've never figured out who that guy was in the background.

I'm going to hit the rack kids. See you tomorrow."

"Good night," said Kyle.

Molly unpacked her luggage and placed a framed photo of their mom and dad on the bureau. She ran her fingers over the faces of Cherry and RJ, tears began streaming down her face. She whispered to herself.

"Mom, am I really built for this? Speak to me dad. I need your shoulder to help me through this."

Just then Kyle stood in the doorway.

"I miss them too. I miss moms gentle touch and dad's firm guidance. Honestly Molly, they gave us both what we need to get the job down. We're going to have to reach down deep to pull it out. It's there, the strength and steadiness that will bring us through. I love you, Molly. See you in the morning. We are here together, don't forget that."

"Yes Kyle, I understand. Your words are helpful. The Lord will guide us and protect us. Someday we will all be together again. I can feel it in my spirit. Good night, Kyle, sleep well."

The alarm rang a blaring sound. Kyle and Molly both jumped up and got ready.

"Be sure you put on your good work boots Molly," Kyle cautioned her.

"I got this Kyle. You just take care of your own knitting," she barked back at him.

"There's the Molly I know, gusto and verve. Let's go get some of that breakfast. Smells good."

They found their way down to the huge dining table. Everything was laid out buffet style. They grabbed some plates and filled them to the brim.

"Coffee anyone," chirped the cook.

"You bet," echoed a chorus of voices.

He came around the table with the pot in hand and delivered the aromatic goods to every waiting cup.

"Oh my gosh," said Molly. "This is so good."

Kyle was busy shoveling it down, he just grinned at her and kept chewing.

They finished their meal and grabbed their gear and waited at the gate by the barn for Gretchen and Ralph to appear.

"How's it going kids," said Ralph. "You ready for this? Here's a handgun that shoots 410 shotgun shells for each of you. Holster it so its steady and safe. We'll do some practicing later today to make sure you can handle it. Looks like you have all the right stuff for the day.

We'll be going out to the south forty acres to search for any new calves that need tending and also for any cattle with any sign of sickness or injury. We are going to ride out there in a utility vehicle. Sorry if you thought we were going to ride horses. We leave that cowboy stuff to the riders. You will get your turn to ride if you want to in your downtime.

Load up, as soon as Gretchen gets here, we're off."

They loaded in and buckled up. Gretchen opened the back doors and loaded several containers with what looked like medical supplies. Pike and Scout, the Jack Russel pups, jumped in as well. She slammed the door and came around and got in the driver's seat.

"Ready, set, go," she chirped cheerfully.

Off they went zooming down the road into the south fields.

"Checklist, water, guns, adventure food, work boots, hat, sun screen, walkie talkies, weather radios, a good attitude, and a sense of humor, everyone all in?"

"Got it," echoed everyone.

The trip to the south forty took a good hour, as the south forty was south of some other south forties.

Kyle was thinking to himself. How many south forties are there?

They arrived at their destination and unpacked their necessities. Molly observed that the cattle were still and appeared well fed and hydrated. Pike and Scout jumped out and started searching the herd.

"What are they doing," asked Kyle.

"The pups?" replied Ralph.

"Yeah, what are they doing, won't they scare the cattle?"

"Nah, they're ok. They are searching for sick or injured cattle. They have been trained to scan and sniff out any type of wound or illness from the herd. They can also do some cutting if we need to get to a calf or something. They're pretty awesome, also they can alert us of any danger close. Like coyotes or pumas or snakes, etc. Scout came up the other day dragging a tarantula. I wish he wouldn't do that; they still creep me out."

They split up, Molly and Ralph, Kyle and Gretchen and started scanning the ear tags of the cattle. If there was a history of injury or illness it would pop up on the read out for that animal.

There were about two hundred head on this plot. After about three hours they had covered the majority of the herd and took a water break.

"So...what do you think so far?" Gretchen asked Kyle.

"Not a whole lot different from home. We have a small operation with a few head of cattle, lambs, goats, and such. We farm about one hundred twenty acres for feed. Molly and myself have worked with the barn animals since we were old enough to carry the bottles for the babies. This of course is on a much grander scale and machine like in operation.

I'm not sure yet if this is a full-time livelihood for me. I intend to learn everything I can and keep an open mind. There are some large operations close to home that run from feed yards to race horse farms. There are also a lot of local farmers and ranchers that just need day to day or occasional help. I think we could stay busy with just that.

This is interesting and I can see why you would like it. You can see the entire sky here."

"If you think this is impressive, come out here at night when there's no moon. I swear it feels like you can just reach up and grab a handful of stars.

Ok, guys, break over. There are some cattle on a plot east of here that need tending. When we're done with them, we'll head back."

They loaded back in the utility vehicle. Scout and Pike had done a good job of finding a few injured cattle and stood guard while Ralph and Gretchen fixed them up. There were a couple of new calves that they tagged and checked for any issues.

They drove over to the next field and whatever peace there was in the one field they had just left; this one was in a state of chaos.

"What's going on here," questioned an excited Gretchen.

She and Ralph jumped out of the vehicle followed by Scout and Pike.

"Stay here," she hollered at Molly and Kyle.

They watched as they cautiously approached the scattered herd.

"Hey, what do you think you're doing?" Ralph hollered out to someone on the far side of the field.

He pulled his gun and ran over to the fence line where three men were trying to load some cattle in a trailer.

"Stop there or I will be shooting," he yelled.

Gretchen flanked them on the left side. The cattle moved out of the way and scattered.

"G-Force to Base, got some cattle thieves on the east range. Send help now, call the Sheriff too. We have em pinned for now. Get here fast."

The men raised their hands and stood there with blank looks on their faces.

"What on earth possessed you to think this was, ok?" said Ralph.

"Don't all of you talk at once. Oh...I know you; I've seen you around town some lately. Do you work for somebody or are you just out for a cruise about town and decided to swipe a few head of cattle?"

Just then a helicopter swept in and landed with four deputies loaded for bear jumping out.

"We got this Gretchen, Ralph. Let's go guys."

They lined them up and held them until the wagon showed up to haul them off to the pokey.

Ralph and Gretchen came back over to the UV and started collecting their equipment.

"Still got a job to do kids. Let's get with it."

Scout and Pike started herding the cattle into a corner, the cattle protested mildly but made their way back.

The rustlers had injured a couple of the cows trying to wrangle them into the trailer. They fixed them up and found another few that needed some medicine for a kind of rash or other that they had got into.

"They must have got into some weeds or something toxic," said Ralph.

The kids helped get them all scanned and meds updated. Pike and Scout rounded up the strays and they got doctored up as well.

"The range hands will be here shortly to get that truck and trailer out of here and fix the fence. We may need to put some perimeter monitors out here to keep an eye out.

Ok guys, lets load up."

Gretchen drove them up over a bluff to a scenic lookout.

"Let's eat our lunch here."

"Wow, that was pretty awesome," Molly said to Ralph.

"It doesn't happen often, but it does happen. We have some state-of-the-art monitoring equipment and will be getting some drones this week to scout the ranch on a daily basis in the near future.

"What's this we're eating," said Kyle.

"Oh, that's smoked bologna. Little barbecue sauce, mustard, couple of pickles. It's a gourmet meal around here," said Ralph.

"I'm sold," said Molly.

"Me too," said Kyle.

"Hey, if you don't mind me asking, what school did you guys go to?"

"You want to answer that, Gretchen?" said Ralph.

"We apprenticed under a licensed Veterinarian some twenty or so years ago. We attended some courses and got our Med Tech certifications. Mostly we learned on the job, and it has been a good one. Ballard pays us well and we have all the benefits of any regular job. If we need advanced surgical help, we have some people we can call and get in here quickly."

"That's awesome," said Molly. "Also, if you don't mind me asking, are you guys together, like boyfriend girlfriend together?"

"Well, I don't know about Gretchen, but I'm a steadfast bachelor. If I were married to anyone or anything I'd say it's our work here. I get all the satisfaction and companionship I need right here."

Gretchen chuckled. "I'm married to one of the wranglers, we keep our relationship on the down low. Our home is in town on the weekends and when we're both off work."

"Come on kids, finish up, we have one more stop to make and then you are free to go about the yard," said Gretchen.

They drove into town and parked in front of an office building. Gretchen went inside taking some equipment with her.

"What's she doing now?" asked Molly.

"She's downloading all the updated files to the servers. Then we will go over to the supply house and get some meds for some new lambs coming in this week," said Ralph.

"Lambs!" said Molly. "Lambs are my specialty."

Gretchen, Ralph, Molly and Kyle made their way back to the ranch house and unloaded their gear.

"Why do you lug around so much stuff that you never seem to use?" said Kyle.

"Well," said Gretchen. "We carry all the things we need for animal care. The other stuff, as you call it, all has its purpose. When we go outbound for more than an hour, we carry lifesaving equipment such as fire blankets, extinguishers, weather radios, walkie talkies, lightning detectors, an array of self-defense items from paint ball guns to shotguns.

Depending on what time of the year, the weather can change very quickly. That's one reason we never get farther away from the UV than about one hundred yards. Over the years I've escaped numerous wild fires. Several twisters, and dozens of severe storms with large hail and extreme lightning.

We've been attacked by bandits, bears, pumas, coyotes, snakes, hawks, eagles, and scorpions. A well-placed paint ball can discourage a wild animal from curiosity and possible aggression. We try not to kill wild life unless it's threatening our lives or our stock.

We've built up our supply of survival gear over the years from learning things the hard way. The fire blankets came in handy one year when the ground was so dry you kicked up a cloud of dust every time you took a step. We experienced a dry lightning storm one year that lite the prairie up from all directions. Everywhere you looked a fire was coming at us. The fires raced at us with blinding speed. We ran for the UV but it exploded before we got there. We hit a low spot in the ground and covered up with the fire blankets.

Other than the long walk back to the ranch house, we were ok. We carry the first aid equipment because an injury or snake bite can turn bad really quickly. Fortunately for us, most of the time, the hardest thing to do is remember to recycle the expired stuff. Believe me when I say, that's also why we work in pairs. You go out alone, you might not make it back. Just like those bandits we dealt with today. If there were just one of us, they could have got the upper hand, or got off with a lot of our prized animals."

"Wow, us living close to town we didn't need to keep much gear close by. It makes perfect sense out here."

"Let's go in and get cleaned up for dinner guys."

Later they all gathered for the evening meal. There were some choices, roast chicken, roast beef, hamburgers, and mashed potatoes gravy and biscuits.

"I think I will have some of everything," cheered a happy Molly. "I'm starved. This looks incredible."

"My feelings exactly," said Kyle.

"Dig in then," said Ballard. "Tomorrow is the cook's night off. We take that time to go into town and eat at one of the local restaurants."

"Say, Mr. Ballard," quizzed Molly. "Is there a Mrs. Ballard?"

"Indeed, there is Molly. She's on a business trip right now. Her name is Lisa and she does all the buying for the ranch. She goes to the stockyards from all over the southwest and selects the best prime animals that money can buy. She has selected the animals that you have shown with your school for the past ten years. Your dad comes down here and picks them up. You get the best of the best to work with."

"Wow, I never knew that," said Kyle. "When will she be back?"

"Lisa will be here by the weekend. Next week we have a load of lambs as well as several hundred Angus and Hereford cattle coming in. I believe she has also found us some new prize bulls. You will get acquainted with them soon enough."

"Bulls," said a startled Molly.

"Why yes, you will see how the operation works and what to do and not do. The hands-on work goes to the wranglers. The veterinarians mix the proper meds and vitamins and supplements for their optimum growth. It's a huge part of what we do here.

I understand you want to work with the lambs. They will get your full attention in a few days. Next week I will show you the work I do in regards to management of the land and all its assets, including the constantly varying animal herds. I also handle the payroll for the operation. You will get a paycheck next week as well. Most of which will go into your scholarship funds. We'll make sure you get some fun and shopping money too."

"Cool," said Kyle. "I completely forgot we got paid too. That's awesome. I've got my eye on a new cowboy hat."

"Lights out at nine o'clock sharp guys. It's another busy day tomorrow. If you want, you can wander outside in the fenced in area where the swimming pool is and wait for the stars to come out. There is sweet tea on tap out there and popcorn if you desire. Good evening kids, see you tomorrow for breakfast."

"Goodnight, Mr. Ballard."

"I'm going to go check out that popcorn machine before I turn in," said Kyle.

"I'm going to go take a long hot bath," said Molly. "See you in the morning Kyle."

The next day brought new training adventures to learn from.

"Coyotes are a pain in the neck, if you get my meaning. We've developed many useful ways to deal with them, but they remain plentiful and relentless. Today we use Scout and Pike to track the entry point for the devils. There is a spot on the western range that seems to be a doorway to their habitat.

We don't kill them unless there is not any other way to handle them. Scout and Pike run the fence line and will hit on their latest attempt to invade our territory.

We're taking two UVs today; one goes south and the other north. We check in regularly and will break around one o'clock. Take all your survival gear and your offensive and defensive weapons. Remember if you actually see one or more. Simply fire off a volley of paint balls or pepper balls at them, that usually scares them off for a while.

We will also be checking on the other predator defense mechanisms as well to make sure they are in good shape.

Saddle up kids," said Gretchen. "See you at noon Ralph...Molly. Have a good day."

Ralph and Molly drove out of the parking area and headed west along a dirt road that wound around for a couple of miles until they came to an area where the fence made a corner.

"What did she mean, other predator defense mechanisms?" asked Molly.

Ralph chuckled. "Ah...she is talking about Dolly and Sid on this part of the range. Abner and Slick on the south side."

"What, who are they?"

"Dolly and Abner are donkeys, Sid and Slick are Llamas. They are some of the many donkeys and llamas we use as protectors of the herds and flocks. They do a really good job of it also. We don't rely on just one method of defense around here though. Some night soon, we will go into the surveillance hut and watch the night operations."

"I'm almost afraid to ask what that is."

"Ok here we are, Scout track."

The Jack Russel walked the fence line slowly towards the south.

"If everything works out, we should meet up with Gretchen and Kyle in the middle around noon."

They followed the pup as he made good progress. The day went by with no interruptions. They stopped occasionally to rest the dog and get him plenty of water.

They arrived at the midpoint at high noon and waited.

"Gretchen should have been here by now," said Ralph.

"Ralph to Gretchen," he called on the walkie talkie. "Ralph to Gretchen, come in."

"Ok, I'm heading south, they might have had a spot of trouble."

They made their way along the fence line; Scout was still tracking.

Soon they came to a small rise, as they topped the hill, they spotted the other UV.

"Where are they?" said Molly. "I don't see them anywhere."

They came up next to the other UV, got out and came around the side.

"Oh, hi guys," said Kyle. We've been a bit busy. Pike got after a puma and treed it. He really didn't want to let it go. Gretchen shot it with a tranquillizer dart. We called for an air evac to come and collect it. They are going to deposit it somewhere far far away.

We also found some coyote tracks. We laid out some electronic countermeasures along the fence line, motion sensing flashing lights and sirens, wicked sounding things too.

I also discovered that the llama does not like me nosing around the sheep. Almost got a kick out of that encounter. Ha ha, that's a good one. Get it, kick out a that one."

"Yes Kyle, we get it. Can I see one of the donkeys? Are they friendly?"

"Mostly not," said Gretchen. "They're trained to be aggressive to anything not a sheep or a cow. They barely tolerate the pups. Dolly is over by the fence guarding a couple of calves. We can drive over there. Stay in the UV though."

Dolly was not very sociable and started kicking when they got too close.

"That's far enough guys. Ok we've observed what we needed to see today. Let's get on back."

They drove the miles back to the ranch house where they found Lisa Ballard unloading her luggage from an SUV.

"Hey kids, Gretchen, Ralph. Oh, my Molly you are the spitting image of your mom. Kyle you could pass for a young RJ in a heartbeat. So how are you getting on with your first days here?"

"Umm, its big, very big, lots to do and see. I've already learned a lot just in the last two days. The next six weeks should be interesting," said Kyle.

"Molly, how are you getting on?"

"I'm fine, a little home sick, this is like being at summer camp on steroids. Each day brings a new adventure to absorb. I'm also learning a lot. The operation is fascinating. I had no idea how a big ranch handled day to day activities. Maybe a little over my head. I am looking forward to working with the new lambs though."

"Well, I'm glad you're ok. Gretchen and Ralph are the best, I trust them with the lives of many a critter out here. Let's go grab some lunch and visit about home a bit."

The cook splayed out a variety of luncheon meats and vegetables for their selection.

"Yum, my mouth is watering just looking at that spread," said Kyle.

They settled down and began to eat their lunch.

"How's your mom getting on?"

"She's starting to come out of her funk a bit. She went back to work at the clinic this past week. I think she's come to the conclusion that she can't do anything about dad so she needs to take care of herself. I think she will be ok. Of course, if dad were to appear out of nowhere, she would be delighted, as would the rest of us," said Kyle.

"We're not giving up by giving it up to the Lord," said Molly. "We know what the extent of our powers are, and right now that is the power of prayer."

"Good idea, Molly," said Lisa. "You guys do what you are born to do. Your dad and your mom wouldn't have it any other way."

"You guys take it easy this afternoon. Maybe go into town for a bit. We've got a truckload of lambs coming in this afternoon. We're going to need extra hands to get them logged in and stabilized. Be back around four o'clock this afternoon, ok," said Lisa.

"I'm ok with that," said Kyle.

"Me too," said Molly.

"Say Mr. Ballard can we borrow a car or pickup for the afternoon," quizzed Kyle.

"Sure can, take the Super Cab, you can see better and nobody wants to fool around with you in that thing. Have fun."

Kyle and Molly climbed into the truck and headed out for town. It was a twenty-minute drive on dry roads.

"Uh oh, it's starting to rain just ahead of us," said Molly. "Slow down, there's a curve ahead."

"I see it," said Kyle. "Oh no, there's a fifth wheel and trailer overturned over on the left side of the road. We should stop and help. Is there a radio in here? Yes, there it is. Calling Ballard ranch, come in, this is Kyle and Molly in the Super Cab. Calling Ballard Ranch."

"What's the trouble Molly."

"Yeah, we are at the big bend in the road about five miles out. There's a pickup and trailer flipped over on its side, it's raining hard here. We're going to investigate and see if there's anything we can do to help. Send help please."

"Got it, sending help right away."

"Get some guys over there pronto and call the Sheriff to rally the first responders over there," said Ballard.

"You bet boss, on the way," said Randall the Ranch foreman.

The rain was coming down in sheets. It was hard to see in front of them let alone down the side of the embankment.

"Molly, you stay here. I'm going to try and see if I can figure out what's down there. Stay put. Understand!"

"Yes Kyle, I understand."

He looked around for a raincoat or jacket of some kind and a flashlight.

"Gotcha," he muttered.

Cautiously he climbed out of the truck and made his way over to the side of the road. He climbed over the guard rail and slid down the hill crashing into the side of the overturned truck.

"Ouch...that hurt."

He made his way around the back of the vehicles and found a man, women and two young children shivering in the rain next to the bottom of the truck. He could hear animals thumping about in the trailer as well.

"Are you hurt?" called out Kyle.

The woman could barely speak. "Yes, my husband is unconscious, the kids have cuts, bruises, and some broken bones. Please help," she cried.

"Help is on the way. Is anyone worse off than another? I have a first aid kit in the truck I will tend to the worst of you until the ambulance gets here. I'll be back in a minute. Maybe this rain will let up in the meantime."

Kyle scrambled up the side of the hill, slipping and sliding himself, nearly hitting his head on the guardrail in the process.

He opened the door and started searching for the first aid kit.

"Where's the aid kit, have you seen it?"

"Here, I have it."

"Get on the radio, tell them, oh never mind, hand me the mic. Base, this is Kyle. There's a family over the rail and injured. One unconscious and breathing, cuts, bruises and broken bones on the others, I'm going to treat the best I can with the aid kit. Kyle out."

Just then the rain stopped.

"Thank God," said Molly.

"Come over and help me with them. Go around the end of the rail, it's not as steep or slippery there. Meet me at the back of the truck. Grab whatever towels, rags, anything you can find to help, dry them off and treat blood loss."

The animals started stirring more vigorously. They might turn the trailer over on top of the injured.

"Let's get the injured moved away from the trailer. Looks like the truck might be teetering also."

"Move the kids first."

They got the children far enough away from the teetering vehicles and out of the ditch which was rapidly filling with water.

"Can you move, can you walk?" asked Molly to the woman.

"I think so, my leg looks like its broken, I can't put my weight on it."

"Kyle, come help me, NOW!"

Kyle made his way over to Molly and the woman.

"On my three, lift and gently go to the other side of the ditch. Hurry it's filling up fast."

They got the woman over to the other side of the ditch. Molly started treating her for shock.

Kyle wrestled with the fast-moving water and finally got to the unconscious man. He tried to rouse him.

"Mr., hey mister, wake up."

The man started to come too.

"Can you move? Can you move man?! We need to get you out of here."

"What happened?" he said groggily.

The man struggled to his feet. Kyle helped him steady and started to walk him over to the other side of the ditch.

"Come on man, we need to move now."

"Ok, ok, I get it."

He was somewhat belligerent, not unusual for a concussion victim.

They fell and washed down stream for fifty feet or so before Kyle grabbed a tree root and swung them out of the water. He helped the man over to the others and sat him down. The man passed out again."

"Just try to keep his head up, he may start to throw up, don't want that to happen after all the work you did to get him here," said Molly struggling to handle the bandages. It's so cold in this water. May be a good thing to slow the bleeding."

Just then there was a loud crash as the truck and trailer fell over. The animals were none too happy either.

They heard sirens off in the distance. Soon they drove up. Fire trucks, ambulances, police cars, the Ballard folks as well.

The firemen shot a ladder across the ditch and came over and started treating the injured.

"I'll leave you too it," Kyle said to the firemen. "Thanks Molly, you were a great help."

They stepped gingerly back across the ditch on the steps of the ladder and made their way up to the road surface.

"Hey guys," said Kyle. "What's for dinner."

The Ranch crew threw blankets over them and hurried them off to the truck.

"Let's get you back to the ranch and into some dry clothes," said the Forman.

The shivering pair unloaded and ran into the Ranch house.

"I think I'm going for a dip in the giant swimming pool," said Molly. "It's warm and dry here. Does that happen a lot? Sudden showers that just pop out of nowhere?"

"Well, yes it can, and sometimes it does. You really have to watch out for flash floods in the ditches that come up suddenly. It may have rained miles away and the water seeks the lowest level until it runs out of energy. You guys were amazing back there. The paramedics say the family will be ok. The live stock was taken to the stockyard for safe keeping.

You have some time yet before the truck gets here with the lambs and the other livestock. Relax, watch some TV or take a swim."

"All that running around made me hungry, anything left over from lunch," said Kyle.

"The cook will help you out. Go see him."

"Thanks."

Kyle showered off and put on dry clothes. He found his way to the kitchen and spied the cook.

"Hey mister cook, is there any leftovers from lunch. I'm starving," said Kyle.

"Please call me, Chef Piere, no not really, just kidding. Just call me Tad. Yes, I do have some leftovers from lunch."

Tad the cook, or chef, pulled out some bread and meats from lunch.

"Here ya go, young sir. Dig in."

"So, Tad?" Kyle trying to talk with his mouth full.

"How long have you been with the Ballard's?"

"Since I was a kid, my mom and dad both worked the kitchen when I was young. It came naturally to me. I love it out here."

"Well, where's your folks now?"

"They co-own a restaurant with the Ballard's, it's located in town. It's a five-star Barbeque restaurant. People fly in from all over the country to eat there. If you go over to the airport, you will always find several small planes from out of town.

"Wow, we will be trying that out soon. Maybe the weekend."

"Look, Friday is my day off. I go into town and help out with the rush orders. I recommend you go on a Tuesday or Thursday. Not quite so busy. You will get top notch service and a square meal fit for royalty."

"Oh wow, thanks for the meal, Tad. I got to get back. The truck should be here any minute.

Kyle walked out onto the huge patio and hollered to Molly.

"Time to get out girl. The truck will be here any minute."

"Ok, this is great. Just the right temperature."

Kyle handed her a towel.

This has been interesting so far; don't you think Molly?"

"Sure, I still have a lot to absorb and keep my other feelings aside. It's a great big place with lots of people to get to know, and lots of cool stuff going on. I bet we haven't seen half of what goes on here."

"I would agree on that. I have some nagging doubts about something. I can't put my finger on it. Maybe it will come to me soon. Meet you out front."

Scout and Pike were dancing eagerly on the front porch. They were ready to go down to the corral and meet the new lambs. Just then a livestock truck and trailer made its way down to the corral. Brakes hissing its coming to a stop.

The driver jumped out and headed to the back of the trailer. Wranglers came out of every doorway to greet the truck.

Gretchen and Ralph were already down by the ramp getting ready to tag the newcomers. Kyle and Molly caught a cart and met them down there.

The lambs were baying loudly in protest.

The driver opened the door and the lambs started streaking down the ramp like they were shot out of a cannon.

Molly jumped up and down with excitement. Giggling like a school girl she ran to the fence and climbed up.

"Oh, will you just look at them," she squealed.

Lisa came over and climbed up next to her. Grinning ear to ear, like a new mother.

"I just love the babies," she said.

"Me too," chirped Molly.

Scout and Pike herded the lambs into the chute to be tagged and cataloged. The wranglers got them all through the process pretty quickly and sent them into a neighboring corral. They were going to stay close to the ranch house and barn for the next few weeks and then released into a larger pasture when they were a little older.

Molly spent her days wandering among them with the pups looking for any lambs that were ill or injured. They found a few but mostly the small herd was really healthy.

The summer was moving on. They only had a couple of weeks left before they went back to school. Kyle spent his time working with the cattle. He and Ralph went out daily to look for cattle that needed tending. Gretchen checked in on them now and then to make sure her numbers were up to date. She spent the rest of her time working with the new lambs with Molly.

"Your time is almost up here kids. There's one more thing I want to show you before you go. Tonight, we go to the Security building to observe the night operations."

"What's that?" quizzed Molly.

"It's best I just show you, then I can explain it to you in real time," said Ballard.

That night they loaded into one of the UVs and drove up into the woods behind the barn and stopped at the top of a hill. There was a medium sized building with no windows and all sorts of antenna poking out of the roof. A motion detector light came on when they approached the door.

"Leave your cell phones out here," instructed Ballard.

He used a key card and a finger print to gain access to the building. "Come on inside."

Over the doorway was a sign that read 'Night Hawks' coyote hunters. They went inside and there were large computer screens covering an entire wall. The video was showing all sorts of white dots running around a field. Some of the dots were pretty much stationary.

After watching in amazement for a few minutes Ballard pointed to a place on the screen.

"There, see that. That's what we call a predatory threat. Those dots running around are actual coyotes. They are trying to find a way through the wire. The countermeasures are deterring them. They keep running back for another try. That guy over there is operating a drone with the capability of dropping explosive devices that will scare them off as well. Beats sending a bunch of wranglers out there every night to run them off. Eventually they will move on."

Just then a dark figure with a mask on entered the room and went to another door on the opposite side of the room. They lifted their mask enough to do a retinal scan and a finger print.

"They must match or no access is allowed," said Ballard. "That room is for a different kind of coyote chasing. Someday soon you will be invited down to observe one of those operations in progress. We'll let you know when it's time. We will send a plane to pick you up and bring you down here to witness history in the making."

"Ooo, that sounds mysterious," said Kyle.

"Believe me, it is. Ok any questions?"

"Naw, it looks very impressive, high tech, and effective. Wait, what are those dots over there? They don't look like the others."

"Those right there are Bears, and those over on the far side are people, they are about to get a very rude encounter of the law enforcement kind.

"Holy cow, that's amazing. Spotting bads guys from up here, and sending in the cavalry without firing a shot. They don't know what's about to hit them."

"Giving me chills," said Molly.

"Ok guys, let's go. We've got other things to discuss," said Ballard.

They made their way back to the Ranch house and gathered in the main room.

Meanwhile back at the Operations building.

"Hey Quinn, so who was that Angel that was in here a little while ago?" asked one of the air control operators named, Skip.

Quinn was the lead operator and had been with the operation for many years.

"Those two, my friend, are the twin children of the legends, Dr. Cherry Jansen and her husband retired Chief Master Sergeant Roy Jansen. Her name is Molly and his is Kyle. They are about to start their third year in Veterinary school. Both are intent on being Dr.'s of Veterinary medicine. Their older brother is an Orthopedic Surgeon in Kansas City. Dr. Cherry Jansen is a famous children's cancer researcher. RJ or Roy Jansen is the manager of the factory that builds the drones we use here. He is currently MIA after a horrible outbreak of tornadoes across the plains in May 99.

Roy and Ballard were squad mates in Vietnam as Forward Air Controllers back in 72. Roy comes down every year for a reunion of FACs and selects a calf and a lamb for those two to raise and show in competitions. He hasn't been here for over two years. Rumors have it that he is somewhere in Central America, helping people set up satellite dishes, of all things."

"So can you introduce me?"

"Sure, there is a big sendoff barbecue set for Saturday night. Everyone will be there. I'll try to find a way to introduce you then.

Hey get back on the screen. There's a pack of wolves zeroing in on some new calves on the west pasture."

The group gathered in the great room. Ballard sat them down and began to speak.

"I know you guys are still anxious about your dad. So is everyone else. Take it from me. The edge of our seats is worn out. What we can do is help keeping you moving forward with your lives and plans. You did really well here this summer. Well, enough to pay for next years' tuition. I hope you will consider coming back again for next summer."

"I expect that will work out for us as well," said Molly. "I have really learned a lot and enjoyed working with the lambs. I think Kyle feels the same way about the cattle."

"Yes, I feel the same. You mentioned a special visit sometime in the early spring of next year, around Spring Break."

"Yes, if all goes well, we will have something exciting to show you. There might just be a whole new batch of critters on the move. Keep it under your hat. It's just between us," replied Ballard smiling.

"Do you have anything to add Lisa, Gretchen, Ralph?"

"Well, I for one see where they get their intensity, focus, and character. Dr. Cherry and RJ have been a huge influence around here for years. It's been a pleasure working with you two," said Gretchen.

"Me the same," said Ralph.

"I personally can't wait to see you again next year. Although I have been discussing having you, your mom and big brother down for Christmas this year. Would you like that?" said Lisa.

"I think that would be wonderful," said Kyle.

"You guys are off day after tomorrow at noon to fly back to Kansas City. Douglas, Uncle Tom and Aunt Marsha will be there to meet you. Your mother is waiting for you at home. She's getting ready for Douglas and Nancys' wedding."

"Wedding, oh wow, I forgot all about that," said Kyle.

"Ooo, I get a new fancy dress. That will be fun," said Molly.

The whole gang came to the sendoff on Saturday night. There was a huge smoker full of every kind of barbecue meat and vegetables you could imagine.

"Wow that smells delicious," said Molly.

"I've never seen anything like it. I better take a picture to remind me of this day.

Just then Quinn and Skip moseyed over and stood close by. When Quinn got the chance, he stepped in.

"Hey guys, my name is Quinn, I'm the lead operator in the Security building, did you find our operation interesting the other night?"

"Well, yes, it was very interesting. Our dad does something like that, I think his company builds drones like that," said Kyle.

"Uh, guys this is Skip, he is one of our new operators. He was interested in meeting you guys, he's heard so much about you, especially you Molly."

"Nice to meet you Skip," said Molly.

"Likewise," said Kyle.

"Would it be ok if we visited for a few minutes?" said Skip.

"Well sure, I'm sure Molly would love to visit with you Skip. I am going to go find some of that incredible brisket," said Kyle.

Molly and Skip went over to the food line and found a bounty of tasty offerings.

"I just love the sweet tea on tap. That's genius. Don't you think Skip?"

"Uh...uh...uh," he stammered trying to find his voice.

"Yeah, I think you're right about that."

He flipped the spigot down on the spout and tea poured all over his shoes.

"Here let me help you with that," quipped Molly.

They sat down and visited for a few minutes. They seemed to hit it off really well.

The kids nervously collected all their belongings and got ready to load up for the trip home. They went around to everyone and thanked them and gave out a few hugs. The trip to the airport was short.

The plane landed and taxied over to the operations building. It was a small airport so you just walked up to the plane and climbed the stairs. An attendant took their bags and loaded them into the plane.

"See you again soon, thanks for having us."

"Quick, before you go," said Ballard. Will you please give this note to your mother. It's her invitation to come down for Christmas. Bless you all and have a good flight."

They waved goodbye and scrambled aboard.

"Whose Nancy anyway?" asked Kyle.

"Search me, I didn't even know he had a girlfriend. He's been pretty buttoned up lately with his residency and all that going on. Weddings are fun, it will be fun to add more names to the Jansen wall of fame.

So, what did you think of that guy Skip? I thought he was kinda cute. He reminded me of someone, I just can't put my finger on it. Oh well, I'm taking a nap. Wake me when we get close to the airport. Please."

"Well. He kind of remined me of that guy in high school that drooled all over himself every time he got anywhere near you. Wait a minute...I think he might be the same guy. What a hoot. I think it is."

"Oh my gosh, I think you're right. He always made me laugh. Back to my nap."

The plane landed at a small airport outside of Kansas City. Tom and Marsha as well as Douglas and his girlfriend Nancy were there to meet them.

"How was your flight," asked Tom.

"A little bumpy, but otherwise ok," replied Kyle. "Molly is still a bit groggy I think."

"Come here girl," said Marsha. "I need a hug."

Douglas went and collected their luggage.

"What have you got in here? One of those lambs you're so fond of," he groaned.

"Ah...we brought home some new work boots. They're kinda heavy. They do work well for when a critter takes to stepping on your toes," chuckled Kyle.

"We're going to stop for some dinner and then take you on home to Pine Creek," said Douglas. "I want to introduce you to Nancy, my fiancé. She's in the SUV waiting for us."

They scrambled into the vehicle and got everyone situated.

Molly leaned over to Kyle and whispered, "Who's Nancy?"

Kyle whispered back, "Search me?"

The Jansen family has been scattered far and wide of late and Douglas being the busy guy has managed to meet, court, and engage with a wonderful girl named Nancy Randolph without anybody else knowing much about it.

They pulled over into the parking lot of a restaurant about half way home, went in and found a large table and ordered dinner.

While they waited Kyle introduced himself.

"Hello Nancy, I'm Kyle, the youngest Jansen by about fifteen minutes. That troublemaker next to me is Molly. She thinks she's big stuff because she arrived fifteen minutes before me. I try to ignore her most of the time. So where are you from?"

"Nice to meet you guys, I've heard so much about you. I'm from Raytown, a suburb of Kansas City."

"Oh, I've been there. There is a fantastic entertainment complex there that we used to go to all the time. Bowling, pool, skating, the whole works."

"That's actually where I met your brother Douglas. He accidently jabbed me in the ribs with a pool cue. While apologizing all over himself, I managed to fall madly in love with him. He was just so cute."

"Hum, never thought of Douglas as being cute, but what the heck. Go on."

"Anyway, we started dating while he was in his residency and found that we loved being with each other more than apart so we decided to make it permanent."

"What do you do other than entertain Douglas?"

"I'm an attorney for a large law firm in KC. I do things like help innocent people get out of prison and help track down taken or missing persons. I've actually worked on several cases with Marsha and her detective agency. Tom flies us around to places we need to go to that are out of town. We make quite a team.

So, I understand you both are working to become doctors of veterinary medicine. How's that going?"

"We just finished a summer internship with the Ballard Ranch. We go there on breaks to get money for tuition and gain practical skills. We will be entering our third year at the university this fall. Molly is more the small animal specialist where I like to work with the cattle, bulls, and horses. It is going really well. I'm anxious to get back to school and complete my studies."

"When are you planning to get married Nancy," inquired Molly.

"We were hoping to get married this past June but that didn't work out. A big case got in the way. So, we're shooting for a March time frame next year."

"Well, welcome to the family. The more Jansens' the better I always say," said Kyle.

"Really, do you always say that. I don't think so. You're just making stuff up now aren't you Kyle," said stern faced Molly.

"See I told you she's a trouble maker," laughing and poking Molly in the ribs.

Just then the food arrived. The table grew quiet for a few minutes. It seemed that no one wanted to talk about the elephant that was not in the room.

Tom cleared his throat. "Ahem...has anyone talked to your mom lately, as in the last few days?"

No one acknowledged his question.

"I was just wondering what kind of mood she's in? The last time I spoke to her she was nearly incoherent."

"My heart is just breaking for her," said Nancy. "She's in my prayers every day."

Molly's chin sunk down to her chest and tears began to flow from every corner of her eyes. Kyle got quiet and slumped in his chair.

"I saw her last week guys," said Douglas. "She looked horrible and then all of a sudden, she came out of the bedroom all gussied up and spit shined. She was in a seriously good mood as if she had just got the best news. I was sitting there with my mouth hanging open and she walked by me and told me to shut my mouth. Something's got into her. Maybe we'll find out soon."

"I'm driving," said Marsha. "It appears that I'm the only one not emotional. I have a feeling in my bones that this thing with RJ will end well. It might take a while yet. But it will end well. Take heart guys, it's far from over."

Fully fueled up with coffee and burgers, they loaded back into the SUV and headed for Pine Creek.

"We've got some time to kill, talk to us about your medical practice Douglas. It's been so long since we had a chance to visit," asked Molly.

"I finished school and did all my residency requirements. While I was doing that, I was invited to join a conglomerate of Orthopedic Surgeons. I accepted the position and also gained rights at several local KC hospitals. My specialty is fixing or revising previous surgeries that hadn't worked out well. You would be surprised how many hip, knee and shoulder replacements that go wrong. I have a new nick name, "Doctor Fixit.""

"I did a revision on an elderly gentleman last week that had had a previous replacement. The original implant was forced into the femur and fractured the bone. The implant was the wrong size and never set into the bone. His leg ended up being two inches shorter than the other. The man was in severe pain. Every time he picked up something heavy his leg would fracture again. I opened him up. Got the previous version out and put in a new one with the correct size and structure. He went home the next day nearly pain free. Last time I checked on him he was working on his golf swing. I'm good at this, I like helping people get well."

"I'm in awe," remarked Kyle. Truly. You amaze me, I feel pride welling up in my chest right now, I might burst from the side effects."

"Oh, hush you goose," said Molly. "We really are proud of you Douglas."

"As I am of you two, it's good to have you home for a few days. So, what's this about spending Christmas at the Ballard Ranch?"

"Yes," said Molly. "The Ballard's have invited us to spend Christmas there at the ranch. He kept telling us that he wanted to show us something special, it is a big surprise. Is everyone going to make it? It's a fantastic place to spend the holidays."

"We're in," said Tom. "Marsha and I are really looking forward to going down there. We have heard a lot about it."

"We are as well," said Douglas. "We or at least I, wouldn't miss it for the world."

"How about you Nancy, going to join us?"

"Yes, I plan too. The only thing that might stop me is the case I'm currently working."

Just then they pulled up in the driveway of the Jansen home. Cherry's stingray was parked in the drive.

"Good she's home," said Marsha.

They piled out and went up the walk. Cherry was waiting with open arms and gushed her love for all.

"Oh, I'm so glad to see you all. It has felt pretty empty around here lately. Sammy and I do manage to keep busy but it's so nice to see you."

"Hey mom," said Molly. "Here's a note from Mr. Ballard, I think it's your invitation to spend Christmas down there this year."

"Thanks dear, just put it in my handbag will you please."

Molly put the note into Cherry's open handbag where it remained un opened for some time.

"When do you two love birds plan on getting married?" Cherry asked.

"We've kicked around several dates. This Thanksgiving, Christmas, next June. We just need a couple of things to jell up so we can firm up the details. Nancy is working on a time sensitive case so it might get in the way. If that wraps up, we might jump on the next available date."

"Just let me know as soon as you can. Mandy has turned the Lazy J into a five-star restaurant and event center. It is quite the thing. We can host the whole affair right there, reception wedding and all the trimmings."

"Dr. Jansen that sounds so wonderful," said Nancy.

"Dr. Jansen...in a couple of years there will be no less than five Dr. Jansens's, that will be a hoot."

"Five, what do you mean five," questioned Marsha.

"Well, there's Dr. Cherry Jansen, Dr. Douglas Jansen, soon to be Dr. Molly Jansen, Dr. Kyle Jansen and last but not least, Dr. Roy Jansen."

"Really!" she said. "I had no idea RJ was a doctor too."

"Sure enough, right before the accident he completed his course work for his PhD in electronics engineering, he doesn't even know that. Don't anyone dare call him a doctor though, that title is reserved for the rest of us. I am of course assuming he's alive and will make his way back here someday soon.

"Tell me more about him please," asked Nancy. "He sounds like a very interesting person. All I know is that your husband and the kids' father was caught up in a weather event in May 99 and hasn't been seen or heard of since."

Cherry spoke. "He and I met in 1972 while he was on leave from the Airforce. I was in nursing school at the time. We fell in love and were immediately separated by geography and secrecy. RJ was caught up in the last of the people subject to the draft. He joined the Airforce at the age of eighteen. He became a FAC forward air controller in the Vietnam war, I was over there as well as a nurse.

He directed close air support for downed airmen during the remainder of the conflict. He also targeted ground operations conducted by the enemy. One of which turned out to be a criminal organization. We had to run and hide from them for years before we could get back together.

His observation plane was shot down on a DEA mission in Panama, he ended up spending several months in the jungle. We actually have new information that he might be heading there thinking he is headed home.

We finally got back together and married in a glorious ceremony. I finished my doctorate and set up a children's clinic. Roy finished his engineering degree and has worked at the electronics factory ever since. He was a highly decorated FAC and rose through the ranks to Chief Master Sergeant at the age of twenty-four.

He loved to lay out at night and look up at the stars. He even caused the entire first responders' teams of Boulder Colorado to search for him one night because he fell asleep on top of the tour bus and no one could find him. He says the stars speak to him.

We have lived here in this house for the last twenty-eight years and raised Douglas, Molly and Kyle. Our family legacy is one of service and hope for the future for each other and for our community."

"That's really interesting," replied Nancy. "I'm going to be blessed to be a part of this family."

"WAIT JUST a Minute," bellowed Douglas. "You have information that he might be heading toward Panama? When were you going to tell us that."

"I just did," said Cherry. "We are sending Marsha and Tom to Mexico to follow up on a lead that he really was in a hospital there. I have had to work extra to raise money to send them there. No government agency wants to touch this. Once again, we're on our own to solve problems. We've become rather good at it, don't you think?"

"Well, looks like I'm going to join this family just in time for another adventure," said Nancy.

Chapter Six

"The Mystery Continues"

"Have we got our passports and IDs updated?" asked Tom.

"Yes," said Marsha, "we're good to go. Travel money and all the important stuff is packed and ready to go. Is the airplane ready?"

"I need to file a flight plan and gas it up. The six-month check has just been done so it's in good shape."

They owned a twin-engine commander aircraft with a range of over two thousand miles. It would get them down and back pretty quickly. If there was nothing there, they would be back the next day. If they found something credible, they would follow it to ground.

"What's the weather like down there? Any tropical storms to deal with?" asked Marsha.

"There has been some advanced activity of late. There's nothing on the horizon right now. We need to watch it carefully because it is still hurricane season down there."

The flight was routine, taking about four hours. They landed at an airport outside of Cuernavaca and found a car to rent.

"Do you have a map of the area, senor?" asked Marsha.

"Yes, what are you looking for exactly?" speaking prefect English.

"The General Hospital is what we're looking for."

"Here, on the map is your destination. It will take about one hour to drive from here."

"Can you get the plane serviced while we're gone," said Tom.

"Certainly sir, we will take good care of her."

"Thank you, we shouldn't be long. Maybe three or four hours."

"We will be here all-night sir, have a safe journey."

Tom and Marsha headed down the highway towards the Hospital.

"I hope this isn't a wild goose chase. All we have to go on is that little article in the paper from months ago," said Marsha.

"Well, I for one believe we are at least on the right track. We will soon find out."

They found the Hospital and found a parking spot under a street light.

"Can't be too careful, no matter where you are," said Tom.

They went into the front and looked for an administrator's office.

"Ah ha, there's one," said Marsha.

They knocked on the door.

"Enter," said a voice from inside.

"How can I help you?"

"Some time ago you might have had a patient come in here that was unidentified. He may have had memory issues and was also pretty banged up. Here's a photo of him," said Marsha.

"Oh yes, I remember, Roy Rogers. We named him that because he had a child's wrist watch on his arm that was a picture of a cowboy, Roy Rogers. It must have been close because the inscription inside the watch said something like Roy...HBD...CJ."

"So, he was here then?"

"Oh yes, he became quite a story around here. He even fixed our satellite dish and now we have 247 channels. The patients love watching all their football games. He struggled with physical issues due to his injuries and couldn't remember any names, dates, locations, details that describe who you are or where you came from.

We helped him as best we could. He had a lot of injuries. We then sent him to a care facility to help him continue recovery, and work on his memory issues. Let me see, we sent him to Sunny Acres over on the coast. That's the last we knew of him.

What is your interest in him, if I might ask?"

"He owes us money and we are trying to find him to collect. He skipped out on a big loan payment; we are head hunters sent to find him and bring him back."

"Oh, that sounds serious. We had no idea where he came from. The stock trailer he was found in had traveled all over the country. We thought he might have been beat up by a cartel and dumped in the trailer. We actually believed he might be from the south, maybe around Panama. That's where we heard he was headed anyway.

He was so nice and really a great help around here. I actually tried to hire him to do maintenance, he was so good at it. I miss him, I hope he's ok."

"Well, he's in a lot of trouble where we're from up north. We need to find him as soon as we can. Sunny Acres you say?"

"Yes, that's right. Here is the address. Best of luck to you."

"Thank you for your help, ma'am," said Tom.

They hurried back out to the car and started planning their next move.

"That Sunny Acres is a couple of hours away from here. It's getting late though.

"Let's go back to the plane and find an airport close to the place where Sunny Acres is, it looks to be close to Cancun. I'm sure we can find accommodation's close by."

They turned in the car, paid their fuel bill, filed a new flight plan and took off for the coast. It was a shot flight, they found the airport and landed without any issues.

The plane was still full of fuel so they paid for parking rental and rented a car.

"That looks like a decent hotel, let's see if there is any vacancy," said Tom.

Sure, enough they were able to check in and found the room quite acceptable.

"I saw a nice-looking restaurant down by the lobby. Let's get some eats, I'm starving," said Marsha. "While we're there let's ask someone about the Sunny Acres care home."

After they enjoyed a nice dinner, they went to the front desk and asked if there was a map of the area and if they knew anything about Sunny Acres.

"Certainly, we have many family visitors from Sunny Acres. It's directly across the highway."

"Thank you so much."

"That was easy. Let's get some sleep and go over there in the morning. Say, do you have cable vision here?"

"No sir, we have satellite dish, 247 channels. You can watch all your favorite football teams. We love it."

"Don't tell me, a guy named Roy Rogers hooked you up?"

"Oh yes, he helped many people with fixing things around here when he was here. We loved him, we miss him. He was so nice."

"I think I'm going to cry, let's get back to the room," said Marsha.

They returned to their room. Tom fell back on to the bed, his face in his hands, sobbing.

"Where are you brother? We miss you too."

Tom and Marsha enjoyed a good breakfast and coffee. Packed up and checked out.

They made their way across the roadway and entered the parking lot, parked and went inside.

The administrator's office was directly inside the doorway. They went inside the open door and spoke to the receptionist.

"Hello may we speak to the administrator please?"

"Certainly, have a seat, he will be out in a moment."

"How may I help you," asked the administrator.

"Hello my name is Tom Jansen and this is my partner, Marsha. We're private detectives. We're on the trail of a man who owes a lot of money. He might have entered your care facility under the name of Roy Rogers. Here is a photo of him. Have you seen him or did he spend time in your facility?"

"Oh, yes...Mr. Roy. He was here for some months recuperating from some extensive injuries. We rehabilitated him physically and he improved. He still had lingering memory issues resulting from a skull fracture he suffered during what we believed was a severe beating.

He left here and went into the care of a Dr. Price. Price is a noted neurosurgeon and works with patients suffering from memory problems. Last we heard about him he was doing well in his care facility in Belize City on the coast. We thought he must have come from somewhere south as he kept mentioning Panama. We loved having him here, he was such a delight to the staff and other patients. He kept himself busy fixing things and was quite the engineer. He managed to get a satellite dish up on the roof and get it working, we now have 247 channels. I really miss him; we became good friends before he left."

"Thank you, sir, you have been most helpful. Does the Price clinic have a name or anything special?"

"Yes...I believe it's called the Memory Care facility of Belize. It's actually not too far from here. Best of luck to you."

Tom leaned over to Marsha and whispered in her ear.

"Wait just a second, I want to see if he runs in there and calls someone. Yep, he did. I wonder what he said."

The administrator went back into his office and grabbed the phone and dialed.

"Hello, Dr. Price. There have been some detectives here looking for Mr. Roy. Do you still have him in your care? NO!"

"Well, that didn't sound good," said Marsha.

They exited the building and went back to the airport.

"I filed a flight plan for Belize City airport. We can be there before lunch time."

They landed and found some lunch at an outdoor café by the ocean.

"This is almost vacation fun," said Marsha.

"Beautiful out there isn't it. I thought about living in a place like this for a minute. Then I looked outside my window at home and that thought quickly melted away. Still, it's fun to visit.

Let's go find this Dr. Price and see what he's got to offer. I'm going to be straight with this guy about what we're doing. I wasn't sure who was watching and listening at the previous places. You can't be too sure who might have an agenda," said Tom.

They asked for directions from their server at the restaurant. She knew of what they were interested in.

"It's just out of town to the south on a hill overlooking the ocean. It's truly a beautiful place. The doctor helps people that have had brain injuries to recover. Good luck," said the server.

They cautiously made their way through the streets and found the entrance to the clinic.

They went in and approached the assistant at the front desk.

"Hello, you must be the private detectives looking for Mr. Roy. Dr. Price is waiting for you in his office. Go right in."

"Dr. Price, I'm Tom Jansen and this is my wife and partner Marsha. We are private detectives, however were here for more personal reasons. Could you please tell us about your experience with Mr. Roy," inquired Tom.

"Personal reasons you say. Before I go on, I need to verify some of your details. Mr. Roy was quite vulnerable when he was here. I don't want to disclose too much information that might get him in any more trouble that he's already in. Do you have any credentials I can see?"

"Here you go. This is our information as well as...as you call him, Mr. Roy."

"This all looks legitimate. Please state your case."

"Here is a photo. Is this the man you call Mr. Roy?"

The doctor studied the photo. After a few minutes he said, "Yes, this is him."

"Now I'm more than curious. Mr. Roy came to me with brain damage from what I was told was a beating of some sort. He had spinal injuries and his pelvis and hips were out of shape.

The hospital he came from did quite a lot of work on him and got him is fairly good condition. Good enough to come here and work on his brain slash memory issues. That is my specialty.

I did many MRI and CT scans on his brain and found pressure on the left side was compromising blood flow. After I released the pressure, his memory became much clearer. He still had lapses due to a fragment of bone intruding in a strategic location. I was prepping him for surgery to remove that bone fragment when he disappeared.

We worked with inversion therapy increasing blood flow to his brain, very gently over a period of time. We also use a blend of homeopathic treatments that increase blood flow with no side effects. We use Hippocampus, Frontal Lobe, Carbo Veg, Baryta Carb, Lachesis, Phosphoricum, and Sulphur. He responded to the treatment very well.

I worked with him on visual functions. I or my staff would show him pictures of places and names of people to try and jog his memory. We thought he came up from the south so we focused on places in central and South America. When we showed him pictures of Panama, he grew agitated and began shouting the name 'Howard Panama,' we looked high and low for anyone with that name with no results. We began to believe he might be from around that area.

I continued to work with him, over time many thoughts and ideas came to him. He said his dreams were haunted by a beautiful woman with gorgeous white hair. When she came towards him, he felt great joy. When she turned away, he felt deep sadness.

Finally, one day we showed him some photos of places around the Canal Zone region and he snapped. The next day he was gone. We tracked him as he was using the bus system. We tried to catch up with him, just as we were closing in, he was commandeered and pressed into service on a large ship off the coast of Costa Rica.

You see, he had developed a reputation of being extremely helpful with engineering work. We suspect the pirates captured him to use his skills on the ship.

Now you tell me why you are really here please."

"Mr. Roy's real name is Roy Jansen and he is my brother. We last saw him when he was swept away during the violent Tornado outbreak on the plains in the US, in May of 1999. We heard through various sources that a man matching his description was found in Mexico. The reports were vague and unconfirmed. We finally raised enough money to make the trip down here to investigate.

Roy is married and has three children. Here is a photo of them. You can see why he would be haunted by a woman with white hair. That is his wife, two sons and daughter.

Roy is a manager of a major electronics firm in the Midwest near Kansas City. Where they build everything from high powered iodine lasers, to drones. He has a PhD in electronics engineering. He lives on a small farm and ranch outside of Pine Creek, it's a mid-sized town near Kansas City. He is also good with animals and agriculture.

Roy is a medically retired highly decorated Chief Master Sergeant in the US Airforce. He served as an FAC forward air controller during the Vietnam war. The reason he triggered on Howard Panama is that he was stationed at Howard AFB in Panama City. He spent several months there. His plane was shot down during a DEA mission over the Panamanian jungle.

Do you have any information on which ship he was taken too?"

"Ah...no wonder he was itching to go, he was just headed in the wrong direction for home. I wonder what would have happened if I had been able to get that last bone fragment out of his head. He might have made a full recovery. Had we known he was from the US we could have shown him photos of the US. Obviously, it's too late for that.

He will need that bone fragment removed eventually or it will cause him pain and additional memory issues, some could be permanent. As it is now, he has moments where he is totally lucid and then he just kind of wanders off into some far-off place.

It makes him extremely vulnerable when he's like that. He's like a lost child. It's not a leap to understand how he got caught up with the pirate crew. They could have just offered him food or something fun to work on.

The ship we think was the RORO cargo ship 'Tous Partis,' it's French for All Gone. It's registered out of Algiers and operates all up and down the Atlantic and Pacific coast south of the US and North of Peru and Brazil. We have heard that it carries legitimate roll-on cargo and in a secret hold traffics everything you can imagine from people to drugs, guns, whatever clients want moved. They pay port authorities fees in exchange for anonymity so they are working outside the law most of the time.

It will be very difficult to get him off that ship. We have tracked it up and down the coast for several months. It does go into some ports regularly so you might be able to connect with him on one of those days the ship is in port. Here's that tracking information.

You will need a small army to bring that ship to ground. I knew Roy was an interesting person, he was very personable and kind. He helped a lot of people around here get satellite dishes on their TVs."

"Yeah...we've heard that about him. We really want him back. Thank you, Dr. Price, for all you have done for him and for helping us find a way to collect him. Good day sir."

"Best of luck, Tom and Marsha. It's been a pleasure meeting you and filling in the gaps on Roy. I hope you find him soon."

Tom and Marsha went back to the hotel and had dinner and discussed the next steps.

"Tom, this is going to take more resources than we have to accomplish any part of success. We are going to have to pull in some favors from the past to get this done. Let's go home tomorrow and have a family meeting. There are some good heads there and they need to know the truth about what's happened so far.

As it turns out I've been working a case with Nancy that might just dove tail with this one. She has a client that has a daughter that was taken a few weeks ago. What that investigation has uncovered is there is a group that takes the marks and then transits them to the coast of either Florida or California and they are put on a ship and sent south to be sold. She might be caught up by the same traffickers. The intel said there might be a French connection.

Wouldn't that be a coincidence. I'll let Nancy know when we get home."

Chapter Seven

"Taken"

"Hello, how may I help you," said Nancy answering the office phone.

"Yes, we do specialize in finding missing or taken individuals. Your daughter was taken you say. Can you give me any more details? Ok, can you come to the office? Please bring any identifying information you have, recent photos, hair from a brush, tooth brush, recently used items of clothing. Yes, we're located in Raytown. See you tomorrow at 9:00 A.M. sharp.

Yes, ma'am we will do our best. We have a team of detectives that are good at what they do. How long has she been missing? Two weeks, have the police given you any information.

No, well, come on in and we will get a file started and launch an investigation. Fees, well that will depend on your financial circumstances. We do have some anonymous donors that help once in a while, depending on the situation. Once again, see you tomorrow."

File: fourteen-year-old Caucasian female, name: Susie Johnson, 4 ft 11 inches, short blonde hair, 90 lbs. wearing jeans and a sequined t-shirt with a unicorn on the back. Was last seen at a corner drive-in hamburger restaurant with friends two weeks ago on a Friday evening.

Next steps: interview friends, family, get police file if possible. If child had a phone get phone records. Survey any CCTV footage from the area.

"Hello, Mrs. Johnson. How are you holding up?" said Nancy. "I have with me today my team of investigators, Marsha and Tom Jansen doing field work. Bill South on forensics, such as DNA. Scott Marvel on high tech such as telephone surveillance and satellite imagery. At any given time, they may or may not be directly involved in your case. I just want you to know the whole team is on it."

"I'm not holding up; I can barely stand. I cannot sleep, food tastes awful. I lost twenty pounds and I'm chronically dehydrated. This is the worst thing that has ever happened to me and my family. We're the typical suburban family just living day to day like everyone else."

"I hate to tell you this Mrs. Johnson. Your daughter is a prime target for traffickers. Young female, pretty, intelligent, she a gold mine for the seller and then the highest bidder. Please don't misunderstand me. Children, boys and girls of all ages and races are being targeted.

We have a very short window to catch anything inside the US borders. Once outside the US things can get very complicated. That doesn't mean that we can't take and do the job. It just engages a different set of resources.

The State Department and the CIA and FBI keep profiles of known traffickers and their travels. They usually stick to predictable travel routes; it's just knowing who and what might be involved. If they get deep into the Central and South American territories, we may have to employ mercenaries to perform extractions.

Have you the things I asked for yesterday?"

"Yes, here is a sack of her things. I can't tell you how much this means to me for you to help. The police could only go so far. The FBI helped some, but they are overwhelmed with an outbreak of a different kind. Apparently, the border is like a sieve these days. Some are decent people looking for asylum, but many others are just looking to score criminal activity.

I can afford $10 thousand dollars. That's all I had left in my retirement fund."

"Thank you, Mrs. Johnson. That will help. We will take care of the rest."

"Please let me know anything you find out. It's her birthday coming up soon. She's just a child. I need her home, please."

"We understand, Mrs. Johnson. Take care of yourself, she will need you healthy when she gets home."

"Thank you."

Mrs. Johnson leaves the room, the receptionist escorts her down to the lobby.

"Ok everyone," said Nancy, "We have a case. We will access the reward money for bringing in the last fugitive to pay for this. I need a work up tomorrow morning on next steps to finding this child. Let's get with it."

The next morning. Team meeting is held on the current case along with some older ones that are wrapping up.

"So, it looks like the cartels are reaching deeper into Americana for their victims. We recognize some of the characteristics of this grab. They used to stay around the southern states for their victims. The last time we had contact with this particular group they nearly got away with three kids from the same family.

We tracked them all the way to the southern border before the kidnappers' luck ran out. This time they have a big head start on us, depending on how close the police got to them, it might have slowed them down a little bit. They might have had to go underground. I will collect CCTV footage this morning from the area and see what I can find," said Scott.

"I will get a DNA profile worked up so we have that data to work from when it's needed," said Bill.

"Tom and I will go canvas the area around the drive-in restaurant and interview some of her friends. We'll let you know of anything we find.

By the way we just got back from Belize City. We reached a dead end searching for Roy, Tom's brother. We did surface a lead that might help us with some other cases of trafficking towards the south. We found out there is a ship that moves up and down the coast moving legitimate cargo, and in secret compartments they are holding other things, you can guess what those are.

We will need a lot of help from some government agencies to track and board this vessel. First, we will have to have probable cause to board, search and recover those lost things. We will let you know as soon as we can connect the dots. There could be a good payday in it for recovery of stolen goods."

"Ok, let me know as soon as possible. I'm going to do some paperwork to get us authorization for tracking bank records, vehicle registrations and other information," said Nancy.

Tom and Marsha went to interview Susie's friends and gather as much information as possible. What they found was discouraging to say the least.

Next day's report to Nancy; from Tom and Marsha.

From interview accounts, a black or dark blue van pulled up, slammed on the brakes, grabbed the girl and took off in a cloud of smoke.

What little camera footage there was from the area showed no plates or markings on the van. There was what appeared to be someone, a thirty something female on the phone casing the area. She disappeared shortly after the kidnapping. We also uncovered similar instances from across Missouri and Arkansas. It's estimated to be about ten young girls or teenage women have been abducted by the same crew.

According to authorities we've interviewed, the crew collects the women and girls and takes them to a safe house where they are videoed and then taken to another location to be transported to the coast for parts as yet unknown, presumably somewhere in the Caribbean or Central America where there are multitudes of ports where a RORO ship can dock, load and unload vehicles of any size and shape, along with other cargo.

Each location where the victims have been taken usually has lots of teenage girls around local hangouts, and is usually fairly remote or rural. The local area also has limited to none law enforcement presence and has been blindsided by the abductions and have been limited to observation and report to other agencies.

So far, we have been able to follow the crew as far as Mobile, Alabama where we believe they were sent to in a large vehicle, probably a truck container and rolled on to a RORO ship, we believe it to be the Algiers registered 45,000 ton 'Tous Partis,' it's French for All Gone.

We lost it from there. If gossip around the port has it, it's a ghost ship owned by pirates and operated by legitimate looking crews. All paperwork always appears legal. However, the night time activities aboard the ship have attracted attention from keen observers. There are dark photo's circulating of young people exiting windowless containers that roll up the dock, disembark the passengers, and then leave quietly.

This could well be a central point of transportation. Proving it and commandeering it are too different things. The next port of call for the ship according to the manifest in the shipping office was to be Jamica.

We will need help to either intercept the vans before they load into the ship or a way to seize the ship and cargo at sea. Might also be a way to catch them unloading if we can track where it's going. Tom and Marsha out. Returning to Base.

Chapter Eight

"What Really Happened"

Roy got excited when he recognized pictures of Panama. A place where he spent many months in the Airforce. He started south along the coast working enough to pay a bus fare and moving along. He didn't get far when while he was waiting for a bus to come by, a sharp looking gentlemen came up to him and inquired as to where he was going.

Roy still eager and excited to get to Panama thinking it was his home. Said, "I'm going to Panama City, I believe my home is there. You see I lost my memory in an accident and I don't remember my name or hometown for certain. I saw some pictures of Panama and I'm going there to find out."

"How about if I can offer you passage on a ship going to Panama? I've heard that you possess some skills that would be beneficial to my ship's operations. We have many radios, radars, sonars, and other electronic gear that is always in need of attention. What do you say?"

Roy got one of those glazed looks on his face when the contents of his brain shift around even a little.

"I think so, it must be a good idea."

Roy and the gentleman boarded the ship in one of the ports of Belize. The gentlemen's a high-ranking member of the ship's crew, his name was Pierre. Pierre helped Roy find his accommodations and showed him all the places he would need to be to get food and perform his work.

He also introduced Roy to some of the crew members. One in particular took a shine to Roy. Kirk was his name and he seemed to be really helpful.

"Say, Roy, is it? My name is Kirk. I've been on this ship for about a year now. It cruises up and down the eastern coast of the US and down to the Caribbean and on into the Panama Canal and then returns the way it came. Loading and unloading all sorts of vehicles, large and small.

Pierre told me you want to go to Panama. We will be in that area in the next month or so. The ship has several stops to make from Costa Rica, Guatemala, Nicaragua, the Bahamas, and possibly on to Panama City.

Your bunk is close to the electronics bay where Radio communications and other devices are stored and operated. No one is allowed in there unless Pierre says so. I guess you passed the test so you will be around there most of the time.

Do not wander the ship unescorted, there are places where it's dangerous. Welcome aboard Roy. Make yourself comfortable. You will have a work shift tomorrow when we leave the docks.

Roy's brain struggled to comprehend everything at once. Every now and then he would have moments of absolute clarity. It became clear to him after looking over the host of electronic devices in the electronics bay that this was not your normal run of the mill cargo ship. It was either a spy ship or a pirate ship. One way or the other he was going to play along using his spells of confusion as a cover. He did still have memory issues but they were beginning to slowly melt away when he recognized something familiar.

The ship made ports of call in several countries along the coast of Central America. They eventually ended up in Panama City on the Pacific side of the Canal.

"Roy, this is your destination, "said Pierre. "Are you ready to depart?"

"Yes sir, I'm ready. Thank you for accommodating me."

"We will be docked here for seven days in case you discover you are in the wrong place and want to go back north. I hope you find what you're looking for."

Roy disembarked the ship in Panama City and found a map that seemed to be familiar to him. He took a bus into the downtown market area of the city. He wandered around for a time and bought food in the market.

Roy sat down at the base of a large fountain in a square across from the bus terminal. He ate some of the food he had purchased and perused a bus schedule to see where to go next. Just then a man sat down next to him.

"Roy Jansen what in the world are you doing here?"

Startled and confused he looked at the man's face and suddenly blurted out, "ALEX, what are you doing here?"

"Roy, what has happened to you? Why are you here, really?"

Struggling to explain Roy managed to spill out a remarkable story to Alex that to him was absolutely unbelievable.

"You say you are having memory issues but when you see something you recognize, your recall comes back strongly. You didn't remember your name was Jansen?"

"No, that's the first time I've heard that."

"Come with me, I have something to show you."

Alex went with Roy in tow and took a bus to an apartment that Alex and his family use when they are in town.

"Here, look at these photos and see if they jog your memory."

"Oh my God, it's the woman in my dreams."

He paused for a minute as he studied the photos.

"Cherry, her name is Cherry and she's, my wife. The boys are my sons, Douglas and Kyle, the girl is Molly my daughter."

Roy crumpled to the floor and sobbed.

"I exchange notes and cards with your family every year around the holidays. These are pictures from three years ago. The last note I received from Cherry said that you were still missing. I've got to get you out of here.

I still stay in contact with Gary Baker, your pilot friend. He works with the State Department. I will call him and ask him what to do."

Alex dials the phone. "Baker, this is Alex in Panama. Have you got a minute to speak?

Are you sitting down. Ok good. I need your help on something of urgency. Are you listening? Roy Jansen just turned up here in Panama City looking for his home. You might be aware of his recent past with the disappearance and everything. He still has memory issues but has recognized himself and his family in some photos I have.

He got here on a RORO ship that's currently docked in Panama City. What, you want him to come over to the American Embassy? Ok, I will get him over there immediately. Don't tell anyone his real name, oh, ok. Thank you, Baker.

Your friend Baker from the Airforce works with the US State Department. He says to get you over to the American Embassy immediately. They will know what to do.

I didn't think I would ever see you again Roy. It's good to see you. It sounds like you've been in a real pickle."

Alex drove Roy to the Embassy and dropped him off at the back entrance. The guards spirited him in under wraps. No one was to see him come in, or go out.

"Roy, I'm Bill Sayers the Adjutant General here. We are caught up on your situation. We've actually been tracking you and that ship for some time now. Those satellite dishes you installed everywhere are a gold mine for us. We've used them to set up a strong communication network throughout the region. So, you got here on the RORO ship 'Tous Partis?'"

"Yes sir, I did. It's docked here in Panama City for six more days. Why?"

"We believe that ship is a pirate ship and has been trafficking every kind of illegal substance known to man as well as many American kidnap victims. We need someone on that ship that knows it's ins and outs to help us locate, prove, and seize that cargo and put that ship and its crew out of business for good. Can you do that?"

"Well, I have an open invitation to rejoin the ship on its return trip north. I still get these spells of confusion due to my brain injury, but I figured out quickly that that ship was either a spy ship or a pirate ship. Whatever the cargo is they keep it very secret and the handlers are a specialized bunch separate from the ships' crew. The guys I worked with on the daily operations were just normal people. I think if they suspect anything, they keep it to themselves. I did the same. I figured out right off the bat that whatever was going on was way out of my league.

What do you need me to do? I will help all I can."

"First of all, we need you to get back on that ship. We believe it's headed back north to collect a new group of kidnap victims some of which are from your home state and region. Retain your cover as Roy Rogers, man of mystery with occasional spells of confusion and delirium. You absolutely cannot divulge your real identity to anyone nor can you contact any relatives. This mission is top secret and your cover is solid as of now.

Your brother Tom and his wife Marsha have been looking for you and discovered you were still alive. We've shut that line of inquiry down to protect your cover.

The crew that kidnaps these young girls is well connected and could be watching and listening to any chatter related to their operations.

We will give you a satellite phone to communicate with and an IR strobe device to attach to the hull of the ship so we can track it. This ship turns into a ghost ship when it leaves port, we never know where it will turn up next. If what we think is going to happen does, the ship will depart Panamanian waters next week and start the voyage north to Mobile, Alabama. However, it has been known to dock at other locations as well.

We will give you communications details on channels and times to contact us. We need to monitor radio traffic with shore operations and relay the details to our operatives. This phone is encrypted and transmits in short burst arrays to prevent any tracing of the signal so you should be safe to use it. It has text ability with a GPS marker that appears every time you push send.

You will text brief messages and then hit the send button, the text disappears after five seconds. There is voice capability but only use it in case of an extreme emergency. You will need to use it outdoors for it to work effectively.

When it's safe we will contact your family. They will be spending Christmas with the Ballard's at their ranch. We run a clandestine operation out of a hard stand building on his property. We are constantly tracking all sorts of illegal cross border operations from there. If all goes well you will be able to connect with them sometime during their visit. After that we will break every speed record to get you home."

"Ah...ok. I'm all in. What's in this for me and my family, by the way? And oh, by the way, I can tell you why it's a ghost ship. It's equipped with the latest in stealth technology. I know because I designed and built it in my factory at home for a military contract. How these guys got it is something you will need to figure out. I could try to disable it but it has a bank of indicator lights on the navigation panel in the control room. Anything happens to those lights; they are likely to know it was me. The best I can do is keep you informed of the location with this device.

"There is a huge reward for the capture of the Pirate King, Pierre. Another huge reward for the return of the kidnap victims. You and your family, including your brother Tom and his wife Marsha, who are helping us on the State side of things, will be compensated when this operation wraps up."

"Not trying to be greedy or anything but I've been out of work for almost three years now. I bet Cherry has a few bills to pay. We could use the funds to catch up. If I remember correctly Marsha and Tom work to find missing and exploited persons, they need funds to operate that as well so...let's get back to business.

You do understand that I have a sliver of bone interacting with my brain which may suddenly cause me to sort of drop off the planet. It doesn't last very long but it can be a real test of patience while it's going on. Kind of like getting a strong migraine headache. It just has to run its course."

"We understand and will take it into account when we're working the OP. All the best too you Roy Jansen. Thank you from all of those whose lives that are in jeopardy right now, and in the future. Get back on that ship pronto. Ok."

"Almost sounds funny after all this time. Roy Jansen, I remember now, I go by RJ most of the time with my friends and family. You can use that as a code name. No one on that ship will recognize it."

Roy left under wraps and reentered the market where he met Alex. Alex was told not to contact anyone of the family to maintain secrecy.

He wandered around aimlessly for a day or two and then made his way back to the 'Tous Partis.'

"Going to make the trip north with us, eh?" said Kirk.

"Yes, I didn't find anything that was my home here. What I did remember was from my days as a solder on Ft. Kobbe. I will travel north to see if I remember anything from those locations. Do you know where we are going next?"

"Travel manifest says we are headed to the Dominican Republic, then on to Puerto Rico. After that on to Mobile, Alabama to pick up a priority cargo, it is said to be worth millions in pure profit. Don't ask me what it is. No one here knows except Pierre. He keeps the cargo manifest under lock and key.

Welcome back aboard, your bunk is the same as it was when you left. The work is going to be a little different. We have some new hi-tech radios that are state of the art."

"Sounds interesting, I will study up on the manuals to keep them in good order."

Chapter Nine

"Going Northward"

"Captain there appears to be a ship shadowing us off to the southeast."

"Keep an eye on it, if it gets any closer let me know."

"Aye Captain."

Roy listened intently to every conversation, every now and then he would zone out with one of his brain fog events, sometimes they were real, sometimes not. The Adjutant General said there would be a British Frigate keeping tabs on the Ghost ship. It has been moving cargo from British interests throughout the region as well.

He said they believed a large group of hostages were being trafficked north. Presumably there would be cargo going south at the same pick-up point. The OP is going to be to rescue the hostages going north at the same time as the others heading south and catch them during the exchange so the ship can be seized and put out of commission.

"Roy, Roy...hey, check that radar screen. It's been acting fuzzy the last few days. Check it for interference, if that ship is getting too close and scanning us it could be the reason. Check it anyway. NOW Roy," said Pierre.

"Yes, I'll get right on it."

Roy goes to the electronics bay and pokes around for a while. He's already planted the IR strobe on the roof of the radio shack. He didn't find anything technically wrong with the connections, he knew he wouldn't. He typed out a brief message, and went outside on deck to transmit it. "Don't get too close, your radar scans are showing up on their surface radar screens."

"I found a loose connection on the transmitter; it was causing an intermittent connection that vibrated along with the engines. I fixed it and it should be good now."

"Yes, it looks good now. Good job."

The ship continued north and all seemed normal. Suddenly the ship made a left turn and headed for a port not on the list.

"Make for a course setting due north by north west to Nicaragua. We have a pickup to make there."

The ship steered to the new course setting and pointed to a port location on the coast of Nicaragua.

Roy listened in, how did they know to do that, he asked himself. There must be some form of communication not in the electronics bay. He watched the first mate closely. Soon he pulled out a device similar to the one the embassy had given him. No way. They have the same capability as the military to transmit and receive encrypted information. Where do they get this stuff.

He waited to confirm their new destination, went outside and texted it on his device.

"We're only going to be here for a few hours. Get the deck hands ready to receive cargo," said the first mate to the cargo handlers.

Roy watched as best he could to see what it was, they were bringing on deck. A large airconditioned van drove up the ramp. A huge door opened and it drove in. A few minutes later the door opened again and the van left down the ramp. The key piece of information was the air-conditioning on the van. There must be people in there. This ship doesn't carry perishable produce, fruits or vegetables.

He texted, "New load of hostages just received."

The network of people running this operation must be extensive and well connected with the latest tech to run with. These guys remind me of the Bac Thu drug ring from Asia a few years back. Only on steroids. That guy that ran the thing. I wonder if he has any part of this? What was his name, Connors something, Jay maybe?

Roy watched the first mate for any movement towards the comm device. After an hour or so he got restless, the device made a clicking noise. Roy slowly moved over to see if he could read the screen. He saw it flash a set of GPS coordinates and a new set of instructions.

Roy typed those GPS coordinates into his device with the following message.

"Looks like Bac Thu, Connors is active, prime location is Algiers.

Chapter Ten

"The Documentary"

"This is Lea Davis coming to you from Station KANI in Pine Creek where just three years ago a large tornado clipped the southwestern side of the county doing damage at the county fairgrounds. This event was one of the dozens of twisters that is now known as the 'Outbreak on the Plains.'

The aftermath left over fifty dead and hundreds injured. Billions of dollars in damage to property was recorded. Some towns and cities have not fully recovered from the devastation. In Oklahoma City there is a mile wide scar that extended for miles and can still be seen from outer space.

Houses are just now beginning to rebuild in the area where once was a vibrant and teeming community. Other small towns have simply vanished off the face of the Earth. Recovery for some has been impossible due to physical or financial hardships. For others it might be psychological. Many victims report recurring bouts of PTSD (post-traumatic stress disorder).

Nightmares and tremors haunt the dreams and what should be otherwise peaceful and quiet nighttime experiences.

One victim I interview told me that it's the worst when it gets stone quiet. Another told me that the sound of sirens or dark skies triggers her stress. Doctors and therapists across the Plains have been busy helping people cope with the effects of the violent and unpredictable trauma that nature can devise.

Yet among the seemingly hopelessness of the situation for some, others have found peace and are rebuilding their lives, homes and businesses, sometimes with the help of family and friends, sometimes with the help of the community.

The sheer magnitude of the storms in May of 99 have spurred a burst of technology and ground safety measures. The storm shelter business is booming, shelters are also being built in some school and office buildings. Unfortunately, sometimes public shelters are a legal liability as there are no guarantees of safety for those who choose to occupy them. Many municipalities simply tell people, you are on your own for safety from tornadoes.

So, what can a person do to help them weather the weather?

Technology has advanced considerably in the past few years. Radar used to scan every five to ten minutes. Now mobile radars can scan continuously with a full scan taking one second. Microphones are now in use that can detect the sound of a tornado up to one hundred miles away. Warning systems have increased speed and accuracy by magnitudes of ten or more.

It is still incumbent on the population to pay attention when severe weather threatens. Cell phone technology, TV broadcasts, regular briefings at schools and business for weather safety including places designated to go in case of emergency.

Others simply put their faith and trust in God and a hidey-hole in the back yard.

However you approach weather safety practices, you are your own best resource and worst enemy.

Society is looking forward to continued improvement in speed and accuracy of detection and warning with even newer tech such as Drones and Airships. Advance satellite scans and anomaly detection has improved as well.

In other news; there has been an Outbreak on the Plains of a different kind that is confounding the local and national authorities. Border crossings by unauthorize people being brought here for nefarious purposes or those being taken out for nefarious purposes, have increased substantially over the past few years.

Technology has struggled to keep up with the demand for identification friend or foe and boots on the ground have limited ability to stem the tide.

These and many other questions are seeking answers. Who will step up to keep our citizens safe from being taken, or overrun?

This has been reporter Lea Davis from station KANI outside of Kansas City. Be well."

"That was breathtaking Lea, when will it air?" said Lanora.

"It should air in November during sweeps week. I am hoping for it to receive good attention so I can land that anchor job in Kansas City."

"I'm amazed at what you've learned and how you've grown over the last few months Lea," said her father, Darren. "Whether or not it lands you a different job, the work you did can be informative for everyone."

"My producer thinks I have a good shot. Of course, she doesn't want me to go anywhere. She doesn't want to hold me back either."

"Speaking of news, is there anything else going on around here that we should know about?"

"No, nothing of note. Marsha and Tom are working a secret OP with Nancy, Douglas's fiancé. Aunt Cherry is getting on but you can tell she is down a few notches from her normal self. Douglas is actually helping a lot of the injured people from the outbreak of tornados.

There are a lot of people presenting with damaged bodies that are just now starting to feel the effects of being impacted by flying debris. He was actually a good source of information. Post traumatic injuries are not uncommon. When the body starts to develop arthritis and bursitis and various other deteriorations due to being heavily impacted by flying objects.

Kyle and Molly are back at the University in their third year and doing well. Cherry misses them and goes down to see them every other week or so.

Dan and Martha are still working part time with Mandy running the Lazy J restaurant. That has turned out well for all of them. It is attracting all sorts of events.

Speaking of events. I just heard from Douglas that they are going to get married over thanksgiving at the Lazy J event center. That should be a fun event.

There's still a giant hole in the family that hasn't been filled with Uncle Roy missing or worse. I miss him. I catch others with faces drawn and sad after someone mentions him.

Everyone I know is praying for a miracle.

Chapter Eleven

"The Wedding"

"Mom, mom, MOM."

"Yes dear."

"We've decided to scramble a wedding together for the Thanksgiving holiday week," said Douglas.

"Nancy's work group has hit a stopping point in their investigation so we want to stop putting it off and get it done. Can you please pay attention."

"I'm sorry Douglas. I've had a lot of patients lately with flu and colds and allergies with the fall season. I heard you. I know you are anxious to move it along. I don't blame you and I'm with you all the way. Let's meet with Mandy tomorrow and get the arrangements made for your upcoming nuptials. Nuptials, that's an interesting word don't you think, you know that it means 'happy day.' How about we just say, Wedding.

Oh my, I need to get a new dress and get Molly and Kyle dressed up too.

How are you fitted with a suit or tuxedo Douglas?"

"I've got it covered mom."

"Has Nancy got family close by, I would love to meet them."

"She's from Raytown mom. We can go over next week and meet them. They are very nice professional people; her mom and dad are both corporate lawyers. She has a younger sister currently in university.

What do you say, next weekend, Kansas City, Raytown?"

"Yes, please put it on my calendar. I've been a bit fuzzy headed lately. You know, sleepless nights and all that still going on."

"Ok mom. We will meet with Mandy tomorrow. I will pick you up at 10:00 in the morning."

"Mandy, sweetheart how is everything?" remarked Cherry.

"I'm great, what brings you here today. It's too late for breakfast and too early for lunch."

"I just need a coffee and one of your famous cinnamon rolls. Douglas wants to talk to you about getting married."

"UH...I can't marry him."

"LOL, you are so silly. He wants to get married here at the Lazy J event center to his fiancé Nancy over Thanksgiving week. I'm sorry I should have been clearer. Douglas, take over while I update my caffeine system."

"Sorry about the mix up. My fiancé and I would like to schedule the event center for our wedding on the Friday after Thanksgiving. Is that doable?"

"Let me check my calendar, yes, it is, what would be a good time, it's open all day."

How about 1:00 o'clock. We will keep the wedding part fairly compact and then we will open up for food and beverages."

"About how many guests are you expecting?"

"Somewhere around one hundred I would guess. Nancy's family is close by but is pretty small. A sister, parents and grandparents, a few close co-workers and friends. It's just us for the Jansen side. Kyle and Molly of course. Mom...if she can hold it together. One hundred should cover it."

"Ok you are booked, I'll get some special stuff prepared for your guests, I get a kick out of trying new recipes. Nothing too extravagant."

"I can pay you in advance if you wish."

"That would be good, I need to order the stock necessary to fulfil all your wedding dreams. Well not all. You know what I mean," she giggled nervously.

"That's it then. Mom, mom, MOM. Let's go."

"Ok dear. Have a pleasant day, Mandy. You are such a sweetheart."

Douglas packed Cherry home and unloaded her into the house. Sammy, the new Yorkie pup was excitely waiting for them.

"Hello dear, oh you are so excited, come outside and get some air with me," said Cherry to Sammy.

Cherry sat down on the porch swing; Douglas sat beside her. The gentle swinging motion seemed to calm her nerves.

"I know you think I'm losing it Douglas. And you might be right about that, just a little. I see him in every corner of the house. In the barn and I even go out at night and call to him to get down off of the roof. He so much loved to look at the stars.

I miss him horribly. The pain is unbearable at times. My heart aches so."

Cherry held Douglas's hand and squeezed it.

"I hope your wedding is beautiful and your bride is everything you expect her to be. I hope your future is bright and you give me some energetic grandchildren someday. Just not today, I couldn't keep up with them."

Cherry fell asleep on Douglas shoulder. His shoulder was wet with her tears. He sat there holding her for an hour or so. He noticed that as he brushed her beautiful white hair that it was beginning to show strands of grey. "Oh mom," he thought as he watched the sun reach the top of the sky.

He gently shook her.

"Mom, mom, I need to go."

He led her into the living room and made her comfortable on her favorite recliner. Sammy jumped up and curled up in her lap.

The following week Douglas collected a still unsettled Cherry and headed to Raytown to meet Nancy's family. The wedding just a week away now. He felt it important that they should meet.

"Hello, Mr. and Mrs. Randolph, this is my mother Dr. Cherry Jansen. Where is Nancy today?"

"Please call me Rhonda and this is Lawrence," said Rhonda.

"She's working a case that is reaching a tipping point, from what she had mumbled," said Rhonda.

"Oh, ok then. We are nearly finished with the wedding plans. I need to get with her on the paperwork, you know license and such. Mom, the Randolph's are both corporate lawyers here in the Kansas City area. They have two children, Nancy and her sister Caroline. Caroline is at university. She will be Nancy's maid of honor next week."

"Dr. Cherry, we've heard a lot about you and the situation with your husband Roy. Has there been any news of him lately?"

"No, I'm afraid not."

Her face dropped and she went into a deep sullen mood.

"I'm so sorry, I should have said not to mention him. It does not lighten her mood."

"Do you need anything more from us?" said Mr. Randolph.

"No, everything is taken care of. We just want you to be there. I'm afraid we must be off. Cherry is due back at her children's clinic in Pine Creek this afternoon. Good bye for now."

"Yes, good bye," said Cherry as they exited the door.

"Seems a nice couple," said Cherry. "I wish we were doing all this under slightly different circumstances."

Thanksgiving Day came and went. They shared a meal at the Lazy J with Dan and Martha, Lanora and Darren were there with Lea. Even Jed and Jane were able to make it in. Tom and Marsha were on a mission somewhere, down on the gulf coast they said.

Nancy and her family arrived in the afternoon for the rehearsal dinner. They checked into the new five-star hotel up by the Cyan Mountain reserve.

Everyone was jolly and glad to meet and greet. Dan and Lawrence hit it off and spoke of legal things for hours. Martha, Cherry and Rhonda made conversation and tried to steer the talk away from anything related to RJ.

The rehearsal went off well. Everyone in their places. Nancy and her sister Caroline were quite beautiful in the dresses, hairdos' and make up. They were rather bubbly and seemed to float on air everywhere they went. Douglas was nervous but quite a gentleman accommodating all the guests as they arrived and departed.

The dinner was fabulous, Mandy's recipes were the hit of the day.

"Well Mandy, this was divine for sure, I can't wait to see what you've got for us at the reception tomorrow," said Lawrence.

Everyone had their fill and left for their homes, and hotel rooms. The next day would soon be upon them.

Cherry got up in the morning and had a coffee and some scramble eggs which she shared with Sammy. She had a new very pretty dress that matched with the colors Douglas and Nancy had selected. "This will be nice she thought."

Kyle and Molly aroused at the smell of eggs, bacon and toast. They were ready to go. Kyle was to be the best man today and was a bit nervous himself.

"Mom, this is great. How are you today?" asked Molly.

"A bit distracted dear, as usual. Only more so today, and I don't know why. Maybe it's just the fact that your father would love to have been here."

Douglas had opted to stay at the hotel the previous night to goof around with his school pals. They gave him a somewhat subdued bachelor party and had a good time. Everywhere the Jansens' went there seemed to be a gray cloud hanging in the atmosphere. It seemed everyone wanted to ask, but knew better than to.

Douglas got into his Tuxedo. Nancy and her entourage got her into her gown. Everyone started heading toward the event center. The guests were arranged as usual, bride on one side, groom on the other.

"Sheriff Jones, how good to see you today," said Cherry, actually quite cheerfully.

"Good to see you, Cherry. So, you're marrying the boy off today. Never thought I'd see the day. He cleans up real nice. I can't wait for the reception, have you seen that food?"

"Yes Sheriff, it's gorgeous and smells amazing."

The guests were getting seated and starting to quiet down. The music was cheerful and helped set a festive mood.

The preacher, Reverand Sam, called the gathering to attention.

"Hello all, I'm Reverand Sam. I've known the Jansens's for quite a few years and am looking forward to getting to know his soon to be better half. Let's proceed."

The music brightened to the wedding march. Kyle and Caroline took their places at the front either side of the Reverand. Douglas walked out and watched and waited as Nancy emerged from the back of the center.

The crowd gasped as she walked down the aisle, taking her place at the front. Reverand Sam asked, "Who gives this bride away?"

Lawrence spoke, "Her mother and I do."

He handed her off to Douglas.

They nervously smiled and grinned at each other.

Cherry had placed her handbag down on the chair beside her, it popped open and exposed a card addressed to her that she had overlooked. It caught her eye and she curiously opened it up.

The note was from Ballard and read; Cherry, see you for Christmas, RJ alive, working UC for the State Department, maintain cover, expect a Christmas reunion. DO NOT BREAK HIS COVER. She sat there stunned.

Just then Reverand Sam got to the part of the proceedings where they ask.

"If anyone objects to the union speak now or forever hold your peace."

Cherry jumped up and ran into the aisle.

"Stop, stop now." The crowd was flabbergasted.

"Mom, what do you mean stop now. Have you LOST IT?"

"I'm very sorry everyone, something urgent has just come up. No Douglas, I couldn't be clearer. I will explain later. For now, make your apologies and let everyone eat their fill. This is serious or I would never have interrupted your moment. I promise when this business is over you will have a grand celebration."

"I'm very sorry everyone, something urgent has come up. Please everyone, enjoy the reception," said Douglas.

Nancy was confused and emotional as you would guess, and her parents were beside themselves.

Nancy sat down and tried to fight back tears. Just then her phone pinged a text. She looked at it with bleary eyes. Wiping away the tears, she read, "Operation Unicorn is a go, repeat, Operation Unicorn is a go. More to follow. M & T.

She jumped up and collected herself.

"Come on mom, dad, I've got to go now. I can't explain right now."

They hurried off with Douglas trailing behind.

"What is going on Nancy?" he questioned. "I don't know which of you is more disturbing right now."

"Douglas, there has been a major break in the case me and your aunt and uncle are working on. I have to get back to the office immediately."

They hurried off and got into their vehicle and zoomed off.

Douglas stomped back inside and found Cherry hoping around like a bunny rabbit.

"Mom, what in the world is going on?"

She handed Douglas the note from Ballard.

"Sit down before you fall down dear."

"What's going on with mom? I haven't seen her like that in years," questioned Kyle.

Molly went over to her and grabbed her by the arm.

"Mom, what is it, please tell us. Please."

Douglas handed her the note from Ballard.

Molly burst into tears, and hugged Cherry tightly.

Kyle picked up the note and fell backwards.

"Looks like Christmas is going to be a different kind of adventure this year."

"Every one of you must keep this tight. No one must know, his life and the lives of many others may depend on it. We will have a wedding son, and it will be glorious.

Chapter Twelve

"Operation Unicorn"

"Nancy this is Gary Baker with the State Department. This is a secure line so we're free to talk. We are working an OP which now seems to have been dubbed 'Project Unicorn' by Tom and Marsha Jansen who are tracking your client's child inside the US. According to your last text they have spotted her at an intermediary safe house in Mississippi.

We are working the OP from the global side with an operative code name 'RJ'. He has given us valuable intel on where the exchange is to take place. It is currently set for Mobile, Alabama for 5:00 o'clock on Christmas morning.

Tom and Marsha are keeping us in the loop on your operation as they appear to be headed for the same place. If we can time this right, we might be able to shut down a very large criminal organization.

There are a lot of moving parts to this Project, it's going to take a significant coordinated effort to reach a successful conclusion.

We must have proof, the proof that your side will provide with a last-minute identification that the girl, and apparently many others are being held against their will and are about to leave US boarders. If they are taken from the country, they will be washed into the landscape of Central or South America.

There are some significant technical aspects of the operation that are just coming into view with how large a scale this criminal enterprise is.

We need you to coordinate on your end the rescue operations when the exchange is made and just after the authorities move in. There will be a lot of young women that will want to go home. Can you arrange all that? Remember Christmas day 5:00 o'clock A.M. is the zero hour."

"Yes Mr. Baker, I will marshal all available resources for the day of. Are we talking dozens?"

"No, Nancy we may be talking hundreds. Both coming into the country and leaving. We are going to stop both from happening."

"Marsha, are we sure this is the place?"

"Yes Tom, the local Sheriff told me about all the activities that come and go without any local involvement. They use a warehouse on the back of the property to make transfers. The locals have no authority to investigate. The feds need a lot more proof to make their move. I was able to follow one of their trucks and plant a tracker on it.

Also, I was running a video surveillance on the property and you will never guess who I saw. Come on guess."

"I have no idea, Marsha."

"Why are we out here anyway?"

"Looking for Susie."

"Well, I think I found her. Look at this video."

"Oh my gosh, it is her. I recognize that shirt and it fits with the rest of her characteristics. And there's how many others about her age in there?"

"I counted at least ninety," she said.

"What's Nancy saying about all this?"

"She's been in contact with the State Department, they believe they are tracking a ship that is coming stateside to extract the kidnap victims and take them out of the country to who knows where.

She is telling me that they believe the whole shindig is going down on Christmas morning in Mobile, Alabama. They will dock a RORO ship at a ramp location and load and unload their cargo."

"Text Nancy your findings quickly. This is the confirmation that we needed to press forward," said Tom. "What's a RORO ship?" he questioned.

"It's a roll on roll off vehicle carrying cargo ship. Everything comes and goes out of sight inside the vehicles. Some are as small as SUVs, others as large as fifty-three-foot air-conditioned containers and trailers.

The return text from Nancy read, "Great news, timing is getting close, watch for any movement. Nancy out."

Tom and Marsha kept a close eye on the safe house for the next few days. Then four days before Christmas the place lit up and trucks started moving out.

"Don't follow too closely, I've put a tracker on one of them. Watch for it to move on the screen," said Marsha.

"Report to Nancy that they are on the move."

Nancy dialed the phone, "Baker this is Nancy Randolph, our contacts say the cargo is on the move out of Mississippi."

"Have them stay in close contact but not too close, the timing on this has to be perfect for us to get everyone in one net. Let me know of any changes."

"Will do."

"Commander Ahn, this is Gary Baker with the State Department. We've got movement in Mississippi. Presumably they are collecting in Mobile for a Christmas docking. What's going on at your end? Do you have the resources to drop the hammer on the big fish?"

"Baker, yes, we've been watching this guy for some time. RJ's confirmation of his coordinates puts him in our crosshairs. We've analyzed continuous data from his live streams from top to bottom. He is about as high tech as anything I've ever seen since the Bac Thu days. In fact, didn't RJ say he thought Connors was behind all this?"

"Yes, he did. Algiers, he said is the dark web internet hot spot. Can you take it down? The timing must be perfect for this to come off successfully."

"On Christmas day, at precisely 5:00 o'clock A.M. we will shoot down his satellite, oh did I tell you he has his own low earth orbit stationary satellite. He uses it to bounce all his data packets off other satellites, all around the world no less? He also is using a small country banking system to launder all his finances, presumably it's the Algerians.

We were able to run a parallel dark web hot spot and mirror his communications. There are more ghost ships and planes and trucks than you ever thought possible. When the satellite goes down at precisely 5:00. The cloaking device they're using will cease operation and those ghostly operatives will become known all over the planet. The question is Baker, are the other interested parties ready to swoop in and bring this tower down?"

"Yes Commander Ahn, there are destroyers from a dozen navies, and airborne command airships waiting to unmask this devil. The countdown is on, it's now late Christmas Eve.

"Santa Clause might come tonight and bless us with some good news folks," said Ballard.

Cherry, Molly, Kyle, Douglas and Nancy have gathered at Ballard Ranch for a Christmas holiday like no other. Hopes were high for a deliverance of the client's child and many others as well as the reunion with RJ in the coming hours.

They've enjoyed Lisa's hospitality for the last few days. The anticipation of the Christmas morning events has everyone on edge. Dan and Martha are going to listen in on the comms.

"Try to get some sleep everyone, 5:00 o'clock is soon upon us. We will meet here in the great room and bus over to the Communications Center for the big event. I know everyone is eager and excited to see this through," said Ballard.

"I'm scared half to death," said Cherry. "What if something should go wrong?"

"Try not to think like that mom," chided Molly.

Next morning the groggy group gathered in the great room and waited for Ballard.

"While we are waiting let's have a prayer for the success of the days mission. Thank you, Lord Jesus, for a safe and successful mission for all involved," prayed Douglas.

Ballard appeared and worriedly pushed everyone into the bus.

"Boss we just got the following message decoded."

Ballard turned white, "Oh my God. Please help us."

"Final destination change, Miami not Mobile. Dock at pier 21 on Christmas day."

Roy typed those GPS coordinates into his device with the following message.

"Looks like Bac Thu, Connors is active, prime location is Algiers. Docking location change, Christmas day Pier 21 Miami 5:00 o'clock A.M."

The ship is making full steam to get to the new location by Christmas day.

Just then Roy noticed Pierre whispering to the first mate. Roy pretended to go into one his zones.

"Roy, hey Roy...is he out of it again! Toss him overboard, NOW, get rid of him, he's just in the way now," said the first mate to the deck hands.

The next morning the Jansen family group entered the comm center just as they decoded his last message.

Roy quickly grabbed his comm device and pocketed it. He punched in, "Going overboard, off the coast of Belize, last message, get HIM."

The room went silent.

"Ballard got on the headset, "Baker did you get this?"

"I got it Ballard. We've got to complete this mission; we must complete the mission. They are getting ready to launch the missile to take out the satellite. It's still on for 5:00. Baker Out."

Meanwhile.

"The trucks are leaving Mobile. What's happening now?"

"Just received a text from Nancy. Location change Miami dock 21 still 5:00 o'clock. Get moving."

"Ok that explains why the tracker started moving again. We need to gas up and get some food."

Tom and Marsha made a quick stop to get some food and fuel. They sat and nervously ate their food.

"I need to talk to someone, I just don't know who," said Tom. "I have an awful feeling in the pit of my stomach and I don't think it's the lousy food we've been eating lately."

"Call Nancy. Maybe she can explain what's going on," said Marsha.

"At this hour. Let's finish up here and get on the road. It's a long drive to Miami from here."

They passed Pensacola as dawn broke and Tallahassee around lunch time. They stopped again for food and fuel; the tracker was still in sight.

The lights of Orlando were coming into view as the sun started to go down. The caravan was still on target to get to Miami in the wee hours of the morning.

There were about a dozen or so more trucks lined up at the station just off the side of dock 21. They were idling their engines. Drivers were getting in and out of the vehicles.

"What time is it?" I'm watching all this through the binoculars. It's huge."

"It's 4:45."

"I see it. The ship, it's coming in. The IR strobe is visible on the top of the ship.

Call Nancy,"

"Nancy there's a long line of trucks waiting to board. The ship is nearly in position. It's 4:55. where's the cavalry?"

Just then a swarm of helicopters moved in and troop carriers came slamming in and blocked off the entrance and exits. At exactly 5:00 o'clock they moved in and secured the ship and the docks. Buses arrived shortly to take the kidnap victims to a safe location.

"Tom and Marsha moved in with the buses. The trucks doors were flung open and people started streaming out. The people on the ship were also collected and steered to another set of buses.

"I see her, there she is, Susie Johnson, over here," screamed Marsha, as they ran over to her. She was sobbing and terrified.

"It's ok, sweetheart. We are here to take you home to your mother."

There was a woman from the State Department checking off the names of those who were recovered. Tom and Marsha took Susie over to her and checked her off the list.

"Welcome home young lady," said the administrator.

Tom, Marsha and Susie, left the area. Nancy's people were helping find next of kin for all the remaining captives. The dock was teeming with agents from every three-letter agency known to humanity.

The ship was a treasure trove of information and cargo. People that were coming in from other countries were given a chance to apply for legitimate asylum. Others were immediately put on a Coast Guard ship to return to their home countries.

"Baker to Ahn, it's 4:59 are you ready?"

"Yes Baker, the missile is launching right now. You will see a large bloom on the feed in about 30 seconds."

The bloom from the satellite's destruction swamped the screen for a few seconds. Then ghost ships, planes, and other vehicles suddenly became visible.

"Baker to all stations, the cloaking device is down. Move in, where ever you are."

Ahn and her crew made entry to the building where the operative was housed. Oddly enough it was insecure. They walked right in. Connors was sitting there waiting.

"So, I'm cooked again aren't I agent Ahn. You were correct in coming at me from the banking side of the operation, it was the least secure of all the operations I've been running. I've laundered money through that site for a few years now. Everyone from the Chinese to the Russians and even some lesser secure American banks have been a conduit for my transactions. I've built a network even bigger than the Bac Thu organization. What tipped you off this time?"

"Do you remember that FAC forward air controller you hounded for a couple of years back in the seventies, RJ. Do you remember him?"

"Vaguely, refresh my memory."

"He and his pilot targeted one of your supply trains on the trail in Vietnam. You had them shot down in Panama. You badgered them for two years before my team took you out. Unfortunately for us in the mayhem you had escaped. Now do you remember?" said Ahn.

"Keep looking guys, the cypher key is here somewhere. We need it to unlock the bulk of his off line files. Check behind that picture of himself on the wall."

"Found it, a flash drive," said one of the team.

"Good bring it here. Plug it in to my laptop. Come here Connors, look into the magic eye. It will release you from all your ill-gotten gains."

"Ugg. Not again. Yes, I remember him now. What's he got to do with this anyway. I thought he was safely and blissfully a home town guy in the Midwest."

"Oddly enough as the universe would have it. He happened to be in Belize City on a trip and got picked up by one of your crew from the 'Tous Partis,' and was pressed into service as an engineering assistant. While he was on that ship, he found the cloaking device. Ironically...his company in Pine Creek designed and built it for a military contract. It appears you are still very good at stealing military hardware, Connors. He was able to make contact with some previous contacts from his military days and broke the news of the ship's origins and prime communication center's location to the US State Department."

"Yes, that cloaking device and the theft of it was one of my best hacks. I've successfully used it for years and made billions off of it. Tell him when you see him that it works really well."

"Do we have everything we need guys?" asked Ahn.

"Yes commander, we've emptied his bank accounts from across the world and put the funds in a secure State Department vault for redistribution to victims and the rescue resources."

"Connors, as gifted as you are, it's really too bad that you couldn't have done something legal. However not to be wasted, your talents have provided excellent training opportunities for our up-and-coming operatives around the world."

The CIA, FBI, DEA, NSA, military special ops all had a field day combing through the data from the bust. Locations around the world were exposed and taken down. People's lives have been restored, maybe we can keep it that way for a while.

Connors was whisked off to a black site secure location never to see the light of day again.

The screen in the comm center at the Ballard ranch ticked down to 5:00 o'clock on Christmas morning. The bloom on the screen signified the end of the satellite network and suddenly ships and planes and other vehicles of all types became visible. Authorities rushed in from everywhere to seize the assets and collect any kidnap victims from locations literally around the world.

The last message from Roy was posted on the screen.

"What happens now?" said Kyle. "We see the operation was a rousing success. What about dad?"

Cherry was beside herself and had to be escorted out of the room. Lisa and the others boarded the bus and went back to the house.

Nancy and Douglas stood there in stone silence, neither could find a good word to say. Kyle seemed to be the most vocal at this point.

Ballard and the rest of the operatives in the comm center looked at each other and tried to look busy.

Kyle stood there with his fists clenched and his jaw tight.

"There's nothing to be done from here Kyle," said Ballard. "Go back to the house and comfort your mother. I'll be along in a few minutes. I need to check on some things first."

"Ballard to Baker. Is there any news at all on RJ? Is there a search vessel on route to the last known location?"

"We've dispatched several Coast Guard vessels to search for him. They should arrive on station at his last known coordinates by end of the day. All our assets have been occupied in the seizure of the ghost ships. Fighter jets have shut down all the plane activity."

There was a long pause.

"I don't know what to say Ballard. He is or was our friend and if it weren't for him, we might never have cracked the organization and helped all the people trapped within it."

"I hear words Baker; I don't see any actions."

"Ballard you and I both now that if he survived the fall from the ship those waters are infested with sharks. I will see if there are any search planes available to scan the area. Pray Ballard, that's all I can tell you. Baker out."

Ballard left the comm center and went back to the house. He entered a room full of hurt and devastated people. Nancy and Douglas shared a glance. Nancy's part of the operation was a success, her client was over the moon with the results, so that was one good thing to come out of it.

As for the rest of the family, they agreed that RJ's contribution was the turning point in the operation and should be celebrated. After all they don't know for sure that he did or did not survive the fall from the ship and eventual time in the shark infested waters.

"Poor dad, sobbed a stricken Molly. I'm so sorry mom. I just can't bear it."

She held Cherry closely, wracked with pain she went limp. Cherry fell silent and then she perked up.

"I know he's still alive, in my heart I know it. Thank you, Mr. and Mrs. Ballard, for your hospitality, I think I'll go home now."

Tom and Marsha drove across country with Susie Johnson in the back seat. They stopped for the night in Hattiesburg and found a great burger restaurant.

"What are you going to do when you get home Susie?" asked Marsha.

"I want to get back to school after the break. I miss my friends and my mom and dad. I will be staying close to home for a while. I'm still a bit nervous about strangers."

"That's to be expected Susie. I think you are handling it really well so far."

A call came in from Nancy.

"Hello Nancy, Tom I have bad news, your father was not on the dock in Miami."

"What, why not?"

"He was thrown overboard near Belize City by the crew of the 'Tous Partis.' His information saved the whole operation but he suddenly had an issue with the crew and they threw him overboard. The State Department lost touch with him. They are sending search planes to see if they can find him. Keep praying, Tom.

They have not confirmed his status, so as far as we know, he could still be alive. Cherry is heading home. After you drop off Susie to her parents in Raytown scoot on home, she needs you. Dan and Martha need you. Lanora is there and will help to soften the blow as best she can. Good bye for now."

"What is it, Tom?" asked Marsha.

"RJ went overboard around Belize City just before the end of the operation. He had some issue with the crew of the ship, they just tossed him over. No one knows his current status."

"Oh, no. Poor Cherry, I know they were at Ballard's watching as the project was supposed to wrap up. That must have been a hard hit. What are they doing to try to find him?"

"Sending search planes. That's all they've got."

"Let's get on home tomorrow, you can be with your family then."

They stayed the night, Tom was restless. They picked up in the morning, ate a quick breakfast and hit the road, arriving in the Raytown area about nine o'clock that night.

Tom and Marsha delivered a tired and sleepy Susie Johson to her mother and father. They gushed over each other for what seemed like forever.

"We're going now, you guys have lots to catch up on," said Marsha. "We're so glad this all worked out for you."

"Thank you doesn't come close, but it's all I have, so thank you from the bottom of my heart," said Susie's mother. "Good bye."

Tom and Marsha went to their apartment and unpacked both the clothes they wore and the emotions they felt. Cherry was Marsha's best friend and all she wanted to do was be by her side. Tom knew that Dan, Martha, Lanora, Darren as well as Cherry and all the kids were devasted. He would go to them in a day or so after he has sorted his own feelings. More sadness added to the already heap of sadness was not what they needed right now.

He did not expect what he found when he and Marsha got to Pine Creek.

"What's going on?" asked a bepuzzled Tom.

"Oh, we're having a party," said Molly.

Cherry was dressed up in her finest and looked beautiful. Kyle and Molly were dressed for a prom. They were getting ready to go to the event center and set up for a big shindig.

"Well Tom, instead of mopping around we decided to have a proper wake. You know, party. Mandy has all the place decorated and Lea is going to put us on live TV. We are going to celebrate the life and times of RJ, aka Roy Jansen, husband, father, sibling, child, business person, adventurist. The man is the bravest person on earth right now. Alive or dead we're done moping and grieving. Should the man ever walk or drive or ooze back into our lives we will have another party, for now we are going to have live music, cake, steak and taters, and root beer."

"Here I thought you guys would be a train wreck. This is actually a great idea."

Marsha ran over to Cherry and hugged her.

"I'm so sorry for everything, Cherry. My heart is broken for you."

"Stop it right now. I love you Marsha, you and Tom have been a rock. Let's get on with life. That's what RJ would want, regardless of his life status."

They all gathered at the Lazy J where Mandy had put on a feast. The place was decorated to the nines. The DJ was playing pop country style music and kids were up dancing and singing along with the songs. The food was amazing. It was served buffet style so each person could come and go as they pleased.

The doorbell rang as it usually does when someone walks in.

"Hey Sheriff Jones, come and join us," hollered a bright and cheery Kyle.

"Well, how do you do; I believe I will."

"Is the preacher here yet?" someone hollered. "Let's get those two hitched while the world is still spinning on its right axis.

"Dearly beloved, oh forget it. I pronounce you two husband and wife. Douglas, kiss your bride. Thank God that's over. I was scared to death someone else was going to jump up and stage a protest. I honestly never had that happen before."

The crowd cheered and shot confetti in the air.

"Mom, mom, MOM, were leaving now, we're going to the mountains before the snow melts and have a nice honeymoon."

"Have a good time dear. Come here Nancy, I want to tell you something," said Cherry.

Nancy got close to her side and leaned in to listen.

"I don't know you very well honey. I do know him, if he has chosen you to spend his life with then you must be pretty spectacular. If you ever need to lean on someone, lean on him first. If you do that most of your troubles will simply melt away. Let love be your guiding light and let love cover your relationship and your home. Have a great life you two."

Douglas and Nancy left in a hail of confetti and drove into the Colorado mountains for a well-deserved rest and honeymoon.

The party wound down and everyone had left except for Cherry and Martha. They sat and looked at each other and held hands.

"Thank you for this, Martha. I know Roy would have had a great time. I know in my heart he will be back and we will do it all over again."

"Sweetheart, if he is alive, he will move heaven and earth to get back here. My faith in the Lord Jesus is what sustains me," said Martha. "Dan is like a lost puppy most of the time. He has trouble sleeping wanting to do something. He's always wanting to do something.

Go home, live your life, get back to work at the clinic. Travel with Kyle and Molly and enjoy them. We are always here for you, never forget that."

Cherry picked up her purse and her keys and smiled like a beam of sunlight, went outside and fired up the 'Cherry-1 Stingray, put the top down and roared out onto the highway.

Martha watched her go and thought, what a silly girl, its twenty degrees outside, she's going to catch her death of cold. She just laughed and smiled. I think we're all going to be ok.

Baker was working on his after-action report. The search vessels and planes had turned up nothing on RJ's whereabouts. Operation Unicorn had been super risky, but was incredibly successful. Hundreds of kids were stopped from being taken. Also, hundreds were prevented from entering the country without proper credentials. Many were eventually accommodated; many were turned away and deported back to their home countries.

Connors organization was high-tech and well-orchestrated. He had hundreds of vehicles in the cover of the cloaking device. He had laundered billions of dollars through the banking system, looking legitimate all the way. He made one small mistake. He bought his tech from Roy Jansens electronics company. When Roy discovered it, he knew the ship was running illegally.

I will put him in for a commendation, him and Ballard's team, as well as Nancy's team, including Marsha and Tom.

There will no doubt be other smaller organizations that will operate in the shadows to use humans as their currency, government policy must align itself with common sense immigration and law enforcement.

I, Gary Baker – State Department liaison declare **Operation Unicorn** a tremendous success, case closed.

Chapter Thirteen

"Hope Rises"

Roy hit the water with such force it knocked him unconscious. The comm device was lost as well.

Fortunately for him, Kirk, his shipmate on the 'Tous Partis' took mercy on him and tossed a life ring in after him.

When Roy regained consciousness, he found the ring floating beside him. He grabbed hold and put it around his neck. He would fade in and out for the next few days. At night he could see lights in the distance. He paddled for a while towards them as long as his strength held out. He knew he needed to get to shore soon or he would be fish bait. Fresh water and land were his target, he needed to fight to get some soon.

When he rested, sometimes he could feel something bumping his legs. He dared not move. He couldn't see the sharks in the dark but their presence was terrifying.

Roy washed ashore on the beach of Palencia Island. By then it was well after New Years. Some locals found him, scooped him up and brought him to a medical clinic where he lay stinking of sea weed and was seriously dehydrated.

The orderly left him on the table thinking he was deceased. He had called for the medical examiner to come and pronounce him.

"Who do we have here, nurse Rodriguze?" asked the medical examiner.

"I don't know, he's not from around here, he washed up on the beach stinking of sea weed. I checked for a pulse but couldn't find one. I figured he was deceased due to his condition. He is emaciated and covered with scum."

The medical examiner had the nurse assistants clean him up. He started looking for any cause of death and actually found him alive. He was covered with multiple cuts and bruises. He suddenly recognized the Roy Rogers wrist watch on his arm.

"Get an IV started stat. This man is alive. I recognize him. He's the famous Roy Rogers."

Nurse Rodriguze, jumped into action. They started the IV and ran him into x-ray and CT for scans. His muscles started to twitch just a bit as the fluids took effect.

"I'm turning his care over to a medical doctor, nurse Rodriguze," said the medical examiner. Call for an ambulance to take him to General Hospital.

The ambulance screamed up to the entrance, paramedics hurried into the clinic pushing a gurney. They loaded him up and screeched out of the drive.

There was a team of doctors and nurses waiting in the emergency room. They sprang into action with the gurney still rolling.

"Operating room #3 stat." Bellowed the head nurse.

There was a bee hive of activity around him searching every inch of him. His cuts and bruises were fairly minor but the quantity of them was a problem. They administered anti-biotics and sterilized the wounds carefully.

They ran a CT scan over him top to bottom. His lower extremities had some contusions from some sort of impact. He has several compressed vertebrae that will need some treatment. There was a fractured wrist also presumably from some impact. His left hip had also undergone serious degradation. The clincher was the bone fragment in his brain.

"Do we have his medical records here?" asked the Neurologist.

"As a matter of fact, we do. He was admitted to Dr. Price's hospital for a skull fracture early last year. Let me see the x-rays. Yes, he still had that fragment when he left their care. It has lodged even deeper into the area of memory and speech. We must keep him here for the time being, he cannot be safely moved just yet."

"Yes doctor."

"Message Price's hospital and let them know we have Mr. Roy with us and he's in a very bad way," said the Neurologist.

"Urgent message to Dr. Price. Have Roy Rogers in my operating room. Alive and breathing but unconscious. Treating multiple cuts and bruises. Please reply." The orderly sent the email to Dr. Price in Belize City. Almost instantly there was a reply.

"Keep him there, on the way with ambulance. Price out."

The ambulance from Dr. Price's hospital pulled up a few hours later. They carefully loaded Roy into the vehicle and gently drove away. Price had instructed them to be extremely careful due to the fact of the bone remaining in his brain and its potential to shift at any moment.

"That was the great Roy Rogers, my friends," the orderly spoke to the staff at the clinic. "We were very fortunate to be able to find him and treat his wounds. I hope he will be ok. Pray for him, my friends."

The ambulance pulled up to the emergency entrance to the hospital. The staff unloaded Roy very carefully and brought him immediately into the operating room.

"Scans please," ordered Dr. Price.

The staff rallied quickly and completed the necessary scans. The bone fragment had indeed shifted.

"We must operate immediately, prep the surgical theater."

The anesthesiologist put him in a medically induced coma.

The surgeons opened his skull and carefully using a new set of robotic hands, slowly extracted the small piece of bone. They patched his skull with bone from his femur and bandaged him up. His vital signs were weak but slowly getting stronger.

"He must remain in the coma for at least four weeks, maybe longer. The swelling must come down before he can be moved."

The staff watched and waited day after day. After 34 days he started to show some signs of movement. The swelling had come down considerably. The doctors agreed it was time to slowly bring him out of the coma.

The process was slow and tedious. They monitored him constantly for pain and any sign of distress. Eventually he was out of the coma but remained unconscious. They began some light physical therapy to help build his muscles. They took him off the ventilator to see if he could breathe on his own. It was touch and go for a few minutes. He caught his breath and coughed a few times settling in to a healthy rhythm.

On day 51 Dr. Price went into his office and rifled around his desk for the card that Tom had left a few weeks ago. He picked up the phone and dialed the number.

"Hello Bud, long time no see, what brings you here," questioned Tom.

They had come over to see how Cherry was doing and take her out to dinner. It was almost spring break for Kyle and Molly. Soon they would travel down to the university to pick them up and go to a vacation spot on the coast where there was a beach and theme parks.

"Come on in Bud," said Cherry.

"I cannot stay, I have a message for you. I know what's going on. In a few minutes you will receive a phone call. When you answer the call, simply say, arrangements have been made."

Bud turned around and disappeared.

"What on earth was that?" scolded Marsha. Does he do that often?"

"No...he doesn't," said a mystified Cherry.

Just then the phone rang.

"Hello, is this Tom Jansen?"

"Yes, it is. Who's calling?"

"This is Dr. Price in Belize City. You will not believe what has happened."

"Dr. Price, what's going on?"

"I have Roy, your brother, here in my hospital. He has been gravely wounded but is alive and on the mend. He has been in a medically induced coma for the protection of his brain. We were able to extract the bone fragment and restore his skull. In about seven days he could be in stable enough condition to be transported if you choose."

The phone dropped on the floor. Marsha scrambled to pick it up.

"I heard you correctly? You have Roy there in your hospital? Alive?"

There was a giant loud cheer in the background, there was plenty of screaming and crying to go around. Dr. Price heard them yelling and screaming.

"It's Roy, he's alive, in Belize City under Dr. Price's care. Oh, dear God. Please let him be ok."

"Dr. Price, arrangements have been made for his transportation. A mister Bud Conley will be there within the week. Thank you so much, I just can't believe this. We thought he was a goner after he was thrown overboard off that evil ship."

Marsha contacted Baker at the State Department. "Baker, Roy is alive, he's in a hospital in Belize City in bad shape. He has been in a medically induced coma for several weeks. We need credentials to get him out of there and home. Can you get that done for us?"

"Certainly, that is great news. We thought he was done for after the ship experience. Never thought I would hear about him again. I will have all the proper documents ready and, in the mail, today. When will you transport him?"

"We plan to have transportation ready to pick him up in seven days."

"I will get it done. I will also pass along this incredible information to the others involved in the OP. He has no idea how many lives he saved."

Cherry was overcome with emotion. She trembled and sobbed with joy.

"Oh, my I hope he's alright. I hope I'm alright.

In the coming days arrangements were made for RJ to go to a spine hospital in Kansas City for further evaluation. Depending on his progress he will be transferred to a long-term care facility.

Dan and Martha took the news sitting down.

"Well, I'll be," said a frazzled Martha. "He's one tough bird I'll tell you that. What are the expectations when he gets here?"

"Well, he is still unconscious, his left hip is a mess and will need to be replaced. His other bone fractures have healed. His skin is dreadfully messed up due to spending days in the ocean. Basically, he isn't very pretty. His brain is the most concerning at this point. They say the swelling has gone down so that's a good thing.

Just then Kyle and Molly came rushing in.

"So, dad is alive?" I knew it," said Molly.

"So much for spring break on the beach and those cool theme parks," chuckled a grinning Kyle. "He's always messing stuff up. He owes us a vacation."

"When will he be able to come home?"

"That's what we were just discussing. It depends."

"On what?"

"If and when he wakes up on his own, walks on his own, talks on his own, you get the picture," said Cherry.

"Bud Conley is down there in the Jelly Bean bus picking him up today as a matter of fact. He will take him directly to the hospital in Kansas City."

"Can we visit him?"

"Certainly, when they get through operating on him and he's stable. You can talk to him and kiss his cheek and hold his hand. They recommend reading to him when we get a chance."

"I'm scared mom, dad is tough but this has been a ride of a thousand broncs," said Kyle.

"What does Douglas have to say about all this?"

"He's over the moon. As you might expect he will be doing the surgery on his hip as soon as it's safe to do so. He will be watching him with eagle eyes. Poor Nancy will have to set up a dinner table at the hospital if she wants to have dinner with him for the near future.

As soon as Bud gets in range, he will let us know when to meet him at the hospital. You kids get some food and beverages, when you can, get some sleep. The next few days are going to be unpredictable."

"Now then, Dan will have something he can do. He and I will take turns sitting with him and to spell anyone else waiting with him. Dan will help him with his physical therapy when he wakes up.

Chapter Fourteen

"Long and Winding Road"

Bud had the Jelly Bean bus refitted for an air ride experience to transport RJ to Kansas City. The journey was going to take a few days. He made it to Dr. Price's hospital, parked the bus and went inside.

"Hello, I'm Bud Conley, I am here to transport Roy Jansen back home. Who do I need to see to arrange that?"

"Oh, over here," said the administrator. "Come with me."

They went down the hall to Dr. Price's office.

"Hello, I'm Bud Conley here for Roy Jansen."

"Good to meet you Bud," said Dr. Price.

"We've received all the necessary documents to make his transfer smooth to the hospital in Kansas City.

All of his medical records have been sent ahead.

I must tell you Bud, treating and working with Roy has been one incredible experience. He has shown tremendous resilience. He has also brought joy and laughter to our people here. I ask you one thing. When you drive back take this route, there are many people across this region that want to salute him for the joy he has brought to them. Can you do that?"

"Certainly doctor, is there anything else?"

"The staff have prepared a banner they want to put on the sides of the bus for everyone to see as you drive through the towns and country side."

"Ok, I can do that. The bus is just outside. Have them get it done."

"It's already done, Mr. Bud. Safe travels, please take care of our SKY MAN ... Mr. Roy Rogers. When you get him home and he begins to awaken he will need gentle care for his mind right now is like a jig saw puzzle with many of the pieces missing. His behavior may be unpredictable for some time. Tell his people to be patient with him and not be offended if and when Roy mis remembers some things, including them."

"Thank you for all you've done for him Dr. Price."

Roy was gently brought aboard the bus and secured in place. He still had feeding tubes and wires connected to him.

Bud started the engine and looked at the map, he followed the instructions precisely as Dr. Price had given him. The bus gently rocked into motion. The brakes hissed approval and he started down the driveway. He looked up to see dozens of people lining the roadway waving and smiling. As he moved into town the route was lined with hundreds of people smiling and waving. It was the same every town he came too all the way to Cancun and then on to Cuernavaca. Roy Rogers was nearly a saint in these parts.

Bud finished the rest of the journey pretty quickly. Once past the border it was a day and half drive. He pulled into the emergency room entrance where a horde of people waited to greet him. The staff gently unloaded Roy from the rear entrance of the bus.

They moved him into a room where he was examined head to foot. Douglas was there watching every move. He reported to the family that he was there and alive. Everyone wanted to see him.

"Wait just a bit before you come down," he told the family. "Let the staff examine him and then make him comfortable in a room. The next steps will be important for his present and future health. I will let you know what room he's in shortly."

Cherry, Kyle, Molly, Dan, Martha, all waited close by. The rest of the family was waiting at home until he got settled.

"What is his current status Dr.," asked Douglas.

"He's remarkably healthy, everything but his left hip has healed fairly well."

"Is it safe to operate on his hip now while he's out?" asked Douglas.

"Yes, I think so. We'll get him prepped for surgery and you can take over."

"Thanks Doctor."

The surgical team got into the theater and prepared to replace Roy's hip.

Douglas asked them to say a prayer with him.

"Lord Jesus, Heavenly Father, please help me as I work to restore my father to health, guide our hands and our skills to greatness. Thank you, Lord, Amen. Alright all, let's get to work."

The operation took about five hours, the implant was a success, however the damage to important muscles was irreparable. He would be missing running and jumping in the future and will likely need some device assistance with walking for the rest of his life. Now they must wait for his recovery.

"He would normally be awake after surgery but his brain is keeping him immobilized for the time being. He is safe and comfortable. Take turns going in to see him. Be careful when you touch him as he might flinch. Also, he is not pretty to look at. The dad and husband we all knew three years ago is a ghost of a man in there right now. We're all hoping and praying he can fully recover and be himself again."

Cherry was the first to go in and sit beside him. She touched his head stroking his hair, thinking to herself, "what have you done to your hair." She kissed his head and wept tears of joy and sadness. Sadness for his condition and the situation, and joy that he is returned.

Molly went in next and whispered in his ear, "I love you, Dad."

She held his hand and cried softly, her feelings overflowing.

"I need you home Dad, please oh please come back to me."

Kyle came in and stood at the foot of his bed and wondered. What can the universe throw at one man and he still survive?

"Dad, if you can hear me, the sky is clear tonight, the stars are waiting to tell you something important, please wake up so we can go take a look."

Dan and Martha each came in and touched his hand and spoke to him, encouraging him to wake up and be alive again.

Tom made his way over as did Marsha, Lanora and Darren and the rest of the family. Mandy prepared meals for them and brought them in as the days wore on. Lea did a homecoming piece for the TV letting everyone in the town of Pine Creek know that a favorite son had returned.

There was a steady stream of visitors for the next few weeks. The room filled with flowers and cards. Cherry has them sent away to an assistive living center for them to enjoy, the room simply filled up again. She suddenly remembered that RJ and indeed herself were legends in their own time in these parts. After all there were over forty thousand people at their wedding.

After a few weeks the visitor line dwindled and the family went back to their lives. Cherry returned to work and visited as often as she could. The staff would let her know if anything changed. He still had a feeding tube but all the other wires and such had been removed.

The summer was beginning to emerge with flowers and leaves filling the trees. The sound of the wind blowing through the trees was comforting.

One day in June one of the staff decided to load RJ into a reclining wheel chair and take him outside in the sun. She rolled him out on the terrace of the care home where he had been moved.

"Say there Mr. Roy, are you just going to sleep the rest of your life away?" she questioned.

"No, he said, who on earth are you?"

The nursing assistant just nearly fell out of her chair. "Oh my God she thought, what do I do now?"

"Well, I asked you a question?"

She stammered, "I'm your nursing assistant at the care home where you are staying right now."

"Where the devil am I?" he hissed.

"Oh, Mr. Roy, you are in a care home near Kansas City."

"America?!" he questioned rather loudly.

"Yes, America," she replied.

"Are you, my wife?" he asked.

"Oh, my no, Mr. Roy, I'm a medical student just here to look after you my name is Betty. You've been in a coma for several months now."

Oh no she thought, they said if he awoke, he might have very mixed memories or none at all.

"I will take you inside now Mr. Roy, there are many people that want to see you and talk to you."

"NO, sit, stay Betty. I need to visit for a little while with someone not a relation. How are they doing, my relations?"

"They are holding up ok. They all miss you very much, Cherry your wife visits nearly every day. Your son Douglas checks in, so does your mom and dad, your brother Tom and his wife Marsha visit every now and then. They are all anxious to see you up and well again."

"Do you have any photos that I can see?"

"There are some in the room. I can go get them for you. Sit here, I will be right back."

Nurse Betty ran into the facility screaming, "HE's AWAKE, HE's AWAKE." Staff ran from all over and looked out the window at the stretching Roy Jansen.

"He wants to see pictures of his family; I'm grabbing them from the room."

"Don't anyone go out there just yet, besides Betty," said the doctor. He is already going to be overwhelmed. This is marvelous news however.

Betty returned with the photos of Cherry and the children and the rest of the family.

"This is your wife Cherry, the one with the beautiful white hair, the girl that looks just like her is Molly your daughter. The young man is Kyle your youngest son. This guy is a surgeon and is your oldest son. There's your brother and sister and their spouses and your mom and dad. That's about it. You have a lot of friends that visit as well."

Roy tried to stand up. The chair was not very forgiving.

"Wait Mr. Roy, the therapist will help you walk very soon. You have been out of it for quite a while."

"The last thing I remember was going over the rail of a merchant ship and hitting the water. I was working a special operation, how did that turn out, I wonder?"

"There are people who can fill you in on that information Mr. Roy."

"It's RJ or Roy, ok, miss Betty."

"Let me see that picture of my wife again please?"

He held the picture up close and smiled and then his whole countenance changed suddenly he became agitated and angry.

Nurse Betty called out for help. The staff came running and helped him back into the facility. They had to administer a sedative to calm him down.

"Call his wife Nurse. Tell her the good and bad news. She needs to know what we're dealing with. I don't know if she can help calm him or not. This is going to be interesting. I've seen memory patients come out and glide right back into life while others ride a wave of turbulence rivaling the worst rodeo bull, kicking and thrashing about over every little thing."

"Hello, Cherry speaking. You what?! He is, oh my. What are the doctors saying? Can I come over? I'll be there as soon as I can. Bye."

"Martha, tell Dan, Roy is awake but he's acting disturbed and belligerent, one minute calm and the next agitated and angry. They are keeping him sedated for now. He comes and goes out of consciousness. I'm not going to tell the kids until things hopefully settle down. I'm going over as soon as I can."

Cherry drove the stingray over to the care home, top down, her hair blowing in the breeze. She parked and looked up at the terrace. Roy was sitting there on a bench.

Roy heard the sound of the stingray as it pulled up, he saw the woman driving it, her beautiful white hair blowing in the breeze. She got out of the car and leaned up against the fender of the cherry red car and watched him to see what he would do next.

Roy stood up, his canes helping him walk. He went slowly down the ramp. Cherry watched him with tears in her eyes. Her heart racing, it felt like her chest would explode.

Roy got to the curb about fifty feet away from her. He dropped the canes and walked steadily towards her with his arms stretched out. She met him halfway with her arms open, they hugged each other tightly and cried, sobbing tears of joy.

He whispered in her ear, "I want to go home. Please take me home."

The staff watched the scene unfold. There was not a dry eye in the place.

Cherry helped RJ back up the ramp and into the facility.

"When can I take him home," she asked. Wiping tears from her eyes.

"Give us a few days to finish up some physical therapy and paperwork. He will still need some PT and memory care when his gets home to Pine Creek. There are people there that can handle that."

"I'm going to take him for a short drive. I'll be back in an hour or so."

Cherry walked RJ to the Stingray and loaded him in. She fired up the engine and watched the look on his face turn to pure joy. She drove them over to Tom and Marsha's apartment.

"Do you know where we are RJ?"

"Looks like the place where Tom and Marsha live, do they still live here?"

She turned off the engine and got out of the car. They walked up to a building and knocked on the door. The door opened and Douglas stood there looking at them with a stunned look on his face.

"Hon, come here, there is someone I want you to meet."

"Who is it," Nancy yelled from the back room. "Who is it, I asked?"

"Nancy, I would like for you to meet my dad, Roy Jansen. Roy this is my wife, Nancy."

"Oh hello Mr. Jansen. How are you today?

Roy looked at her with searching eyes.

"You said she is your wife. Well, isn't that a fine how do you do. Welcome to the family Nancy. I look forward to getting to know you better in the coming days. I'm sure we will have time for you to answer all of my questions. In the meantime, you asked how am I doing. That young lady is a good question. One that is going to be tested vigorously in the near future. Douglas, I couldn't be prouder son."

Douglas embraced RJ with all his strength.

"I've missed you so much, Dad. Welcome home."

They visited for a few more minutes and then Cherry turned and knocked on the door just across the hallway.

"Hello, OH HELLO," blurted a shocked Tom Jansen.

"Marsha, come here and see this," said Tom.

"Welcome home brother."

Tom hugged his brother and shook his hand vigorously. Marsha came running.

"Oh my God, welcome home RJ. It's so good to see you."

Marsha first hugged Cherry and whispered in her ear. "Is he ok?"

Cherry whispered back, "Mostly, but there is still some work to be done. He's started to remember many things by looking at pictures and being face to face with people he knew. He's coming home with me tomorrow. The therapists in Pine Creek are going to work with him on physical needs and memory care.

"Marsha are you keeping him in line," joked RJ. When I get home, we're going to fire up the grill and have a party. Gosh I need a good burger."

"Ok then everyone, I have to get him back so they can process him out. See you all soon."

Chapter Fifteen

"Home at Last"

The events of the past few years have affected the Jansens's world to some extent or another. Each person had a trauma to process some emotional, some physical, and clearly some mental.

The scattering of the souls has tested each of them as individuals and as a family. Yet each of them was never alone. The Spirit of God lives in them and covers them with love. Each has their own testimony as to how it has affected them.

Scars of all kinds are healing; some will take longer than others. Some are invisible while others are plainly obvious.

Dan and Martha grieved their son. Cherry her husband. Douglas, Molly and Kyle their father. Tom and Lanora, a sibling and the nieces Lea and Mandy their uncle.

RJ surveyed the property around their home. The barn was still there, the truck, the animals were all gone, Cherry couldn't keep up with them. She had taken care of the house really well. The new dog Sammy was still getting used to him. She nipped at his ankles and barked for what seemed like hours. After a few days he found some treats and they were able to make friends.

RJ was never one to sit around for long so he jumped on the physical therapy to try and get back some sense of normal.

His friends stopped by and visited once in a while. He could not drive yet, so he was dependent on Cherry to carry him around. Dan and Martha, his parents, would take him places, too.

"I must confess Jackie and Mark. The physical therapy is hard. The left side is so stiff."

"It's coming along Roy; you've been through some serious trauma. We're going to keep trying new things and getting you to use what you already have, regularly."

"I get it, it's just frustrating some times."

Roy met with Carla his memory care therapist three times a week. They practice all sorts of exercises from flash cards to picture books, annuals and magazines. Roy was anxious to get back to his work at the factory. The factory would love to have him back. The doctors have forbidden it for the time being.

Roy loved to go over to the Lazy J for coffee and cinnamon rolls. Mandy has the recipe locked down. People from all over come just to get those rolls.

"Hey look mom, I found this old guitar in a closet. I think I will learn to play it some."

Martha grabbed Dan, "See if you can get ahold of Bud Conley. There is a serious issue that needs tending. Only he can help."

Dan searched for a contact number for Bud. Just then there was a knock at the door.

"Hello, I know what's going on Dan. I will handle it."

Dan stood there with his jaw dropped. He thought, "How in the world?"

RJ was on the porch of the Lazy J rocking in a chair and strumming the twelve-string guitar.

"She sounds pretty good don't ya think Bud? Could use a tune up.

Bud put his hand on RJ's shoulder. RJ fell into a trance.

"Roy Jansen, I am your guardian Angel past present and future. You will remember from this time forth, your childhood, school days, your first car, working at the Tack and Feed. Your military experience, meeting Cherry for the first time and falling in love. Your time in the service in Vietnam with Baker, Ballard and your other squad mates. You will remember putting a band together called the Snake Skin Rangers. You will remember your homecoming and wedding with Cherry. You will remember the birth of your children and the joy they bring.

You will remember all the events around the Cyan Mountain tragedy and recovery, the equipment you manufactured for the agents to use in Germany. You will remember the wonderful vacation in Europe.

You will remember the days working with your children in their school projects with their animals. You will remember all the wonderful times with Cherry. You will remember your siblings and mother and father and your grandparents. You will remember the work you do at home and at the electronics factory. You will remember it all, including being swept up in the cyclone.

You will remember all the good you did across the plains of Mexico and the other nations in Central America. You will remember the mission Operation Unicorn and you will be remembered for the lives you saved and those you changed for the better. Love will fill the holes in your soul and the gaps in your mind. Let the curtains pull back on the windows of your mind and let your life be set free."

RJ awoke from the trance and started playing one of his favorite tunes.

"Say I wonder what ever happened to those Snake Skin Rangers anyhow? That was a fun time back then."

Bud just smiled and said, "Until next time my friend."

Dan and Martha drove RJ home. Cherry was in the house getting ready to bake cookies.

RJ went in the front door and snatched up Sammy and rubbed her head.

"Whatcha' making babe," said RJ

"I'm making cookies."

"Yum, what kind?"

"The lemon kind that you like."

"Oh, wow I love those. Don't forget to make those smiley faces that you used to do. The kids really liked those."

Cherry stood there with tears streaming down her face. She wiped them away with her apron. She thought to herself. "The real Roy Jansen is back."

"Let me know when those cookies are done, I'm starved. Oo ee, they sure smell good."

He sat there with his guitar in hand and played her one of her favorite songs.

"By the way I'm going to get checked out to go back to work next week, it's time. Speaking of the kids, where are they?"

"They are at Ballard's Ranch for their summer internships to earn tuition money. They'll be there for a few more weeks."

"What have you got going on at work? Can you take a break? If I could drive, I would go there myself. I would love to have the most beautiful escort on the planet, if you would take me, please, I want to see the cows. Really, I want to get a few head to graze the ranch for some good beef. How about it?"

Cherry looked at him and fluttered her eyelids and grinned a wry smile.

"Stop that, you know that drives me crazy. Stop it now."

Later that day Cherry was on the phone with the clinic.

"Nothing going on that you can't handle? Good I'm taking a few days and going out of town with RJ. Bye. It's settled, lets pack a bag and go out of town. Better call Ballard and let him know we're coming."

"Good idea."

Phone ringing, "Hello, hey this is RJ. I was wondering if it would be ok if Cherry and I came down for a couple of days? I'd like to check in on the kids and maybe arrange for the purchase of a few head of cattle?"

"Well hello to you, too. This is Lisa, I think it would be just fine if you come down. The kids still don't know you're awake. That would be a great surprise for them. Maybe Molly will stop moping around all the time. Come on down, see you soon."

Cherry and RJ drove the few hundred miles to the Ballard's Ranch. The weather was warm and windy. The blue sky was traced with the vapor trails of jet planes making their way from coast to coast.

They got to the ranch just about nightfall. The stars in the east were starting to pop out and the moon was full and shining brightly. There was a pond just outside the ranch gates. The reflection of the moon shone brilliantly as the water was perfectly still.

"Hum, thought RJ, there's two moons out tonight. It was so peaceful. He reached for Cherry's hand just as she downshifted.

"That was fun," she said playfully. "I told you when we left, no side seat driving buster."

He laughed. "Oh, ya got me."

They pulled into the parking area and unloaded their belongings and went to the door. Just as they got to the door it flung open and a flying Molly thing dashed out and jumped into her daddy's arms. Kyle was right behind her literally jumping up and down like a little kid.

Cherry, joined the group hug, they bawled like a baby calf.

"Come on inside you guys," said Lisa. "Clay will be along any minute. Are you hungry? Tad has some left overs' from dinner if you're interested?"

"Speaking for myself. I've been dreaming about Tad's world-famous barbecue for a long time. We've been on the road all day; I think we would both love some left overs."

RJ went into the kitchen to visit with Tad for a few minutes while he prepared the meal.

Molly and Kyle sandwiched Cherry and started whispering questions into either ear at the same time.

"Hey, you two, simmer down for a second. I'll answer all of your questions in good time. First of all, besides his obvious physical condition with his hip, he's the same ole RJ. Just don't touch the side of his head or you might draw back a bloody stump. You can ask him anything you want. He's tired of being tested though, so be careful to make sure you're reminiscing and not evaluating.

I would advise talking about yourselves and what the future looks like for you. He's anxious to get back to normal, as normal as his body will allow him to be. I think he is interested in some new tech they're working on at the electronics factory, his mind will whirl around that... for goodness' sake. Oh, if you truly want to test him, ask him to play your favorite songs on his guitar. He brought it with us.

He loves all of us, and is getting back into husband and father protection mode so I wouldn't advise springing anything or anyone strange or new just yet. If there any side effects of his time away that I can surmise, it's that he's a little suspicious of strangers and his confidence seems to ebb and flow. His memory seems fine now, it's his emotional self-that's still mending. If you have any changes you want to bring up do it gradually. One minute he's the same old dad and then he can suddenly become the child that still lives in there too.

Remember he's missed out on three years of our lives and he wants to squeeze the catchup bottle pretty hard. I told him not to hard or it will splash out all over, you don't want that. He seems to understand. His eyes light up every time he sees someone from the past or a friend. His eyes light up every time he sees me. I never want to get used to that. One of the most wonderful things about him is his childlike expressions when he sees someone or something he loves.

Sit next to him when you get a chance and watch his facial expression and you will know what I mean. On the other hand, if he's had a problem with something or someone, he doesn't like, he doesn't hold back on that either. If there is no expression on his face, he's studying something. That...is the same old RJ."

RJ visited with Tad for a few minutes. You could hear them laughing and joking around in the kitchen.

Everyone gathered in the large dining room. Ice tea was served with popcorn and cookies.

RJ found a seat and rubbed his hands together and smiled.

"Cotton Top, come here and sit by me while we enjoy this fabulous meal."

The room fell silent, everybody looked at each other in wonder.

Ballard had just walked in and took stock of the expressions on their faces.

He laughed loudly. "Have you guys not ever heard him call her that? That was the first thing he called Cherry when they met in Sparksdale all those years ago?

"Welcome to our home friends. Eat up."

Ballard grabbed a glass full of sweet tea and stood up and said, "I propose a toast, to the Jansens, reunited, to friends reunited, to a safer and better world to live in."

"AMEN brother," said RJ.

"Since we're all here, well mostly all here. I've been authorized to confer some credentials that have been a long time coming. RJ, please stand. I hereby confer the certificate of Doctorate of Electronics Engineering upon you with all the rights and privileges that comes with it. Cherry, you can smash him over the head with a champagne bottle or give him a great big kiss."

"Wow how did that happen?" Said a very surprised RJ.

"You finished your course work just before the tornado spoiled your graduation. You can still walk the stage if you want to. Congratulations Dr. Roy Rogers Jansen."

"Oh my gosh you mean dad has a middle name? All this time you never told us?" said a dismayed Kyle.

"I think I'll hold off on walking the stage. This is pretty great though. Thank you for my diploma. How about we adjourn to the patio. I want to take a look at the stars, see what their talking about."

The group scattered. Cherry and Lisa sat in the great room and visited. The kids went off to their rooms. It was going to be another busy day for them tomorrow.

Roy and Ballard took their ice tea to the patio.

"It's beautiful out here at night. The sky is clear, the stars are bright, the moon is full and casting shadows over the landscape. It's peaceful and calming."

"Clay, I would like to check out the security center you have up on the hill. I'm thinking about some new projects at work that this operation might benefit from. I've been studying this new system of algorithms that can self-operate a device.

AI, artificial intelligence they are calling it. If I can use the algorithms to program a Drone to predict where an invader might go next it could save seconds or minutes. Or a herd of cattle to see how they ebb and flow.

I would like to find a way to program Search and Weather Radar systems to predict the direction and intensity of severe weather including mesocyclone type storms to help provide warning in areas that are not covered by sirens or TV coverage. There are some new applications coming out for hand held devices that could accomplish that, if they are done right.

I'm not too keen on AI running everything from your refrigerator to the vast computer systems used to run government and business. From what I can tell AI is only as good as the programmers and their seen or unseen bias's. If I don't know and trust the programmer, how can I trust the systems they program.

Anyway, I am interested in how the technology can be used for security and weather prediction."

"Sure, we are already implementing some AI in our long-range security scans to help us distinguish between biological life forms. Heat signatures sometimes blend everything together such as in a large gathering of people. It's helping us distinguish types and quantities of individuals.

Get some rest RJ, we'll talk more tomorrow. It's really good to see you alive and well my friend.

Roy stood there for a few minutes sipping his ice tea and drinking in the sights and sounds of the night life. He thought to himself, "This is a picture worth keeping in my mind. Snap, there I go, it's a keeper."

He went back inside and sat with Cherry and Lisa for a few minutes. After a minute or two the photos around the room caught his eye. He got up and started walking around the room.

"Wow, this is like taking in a museum. I remember this picture, it's of the first flight crew in Vietnam. There's a really young me, there's Wallace the Army FAC, First Lieutenant Baker the pilot, and Clay Ballard the squad leader, wait who is that in the background?"

RJ stared hard and looked closely at the photo.

"Holy smoke, I believe that's Bud Conley in the background trying to look away he was, didn't quite make it."

Chills jumped up all over his neck, his hair tried to stand on end. It was like the room suddenly filled with electricity.

"Huh," said a puzzled RJ.

"What is it Roy," said Cherry.

"Oh nothing, thought I saw somebody I knew in this picture. It's all good."

"Let's hit the rack babe, it has been a long day, a wonderful day too."

They retired to their room. Roy fell back onto the bed, Cherry laid down next to him.

"Million dollars for your thoughts?" she chuckled.

He turned his head and looked into her bright blue eyes. He hair falling down across her face.

He brushed her hair back and surveyed every square inch of her beautiful face.

"I didn't want to bring this up dear, but I think you might have a couple of grey hairs and maybe even a slight wrinkle just there around your eyes."

She jabbed him in the ribs.

"Here I thought you were going to spin something romantic at me. Just you wait buster."

He grabbed her head with his hands and kissed her face gently.

"Ok, ok, that's enough," she squealed.

I was making up for lost time. I am going to squeeze that catch up bottle pretty hard in the next few days, get used to it."

Cherry poked him in the ribs one more time.

"Let's get some sleep, you're wearing me out."

RJ was first down stairs to the breakfast buffet. Others gathered slowly; it was after all, five o'clock in the morning. His adrenalin was pumping. He had already had a swim in the pool and walked around the grounds. Not to miss the sun peaking over the eastern sky. The beautiful hues of red, yellow and orange were breath taking.

"Tad, this is simply marvelous. I may have to visit more often."

"You're welcome anytime Mr. Roy."

Cherry sleepy eyed, wandered into the room, stretching as she rounded the big table shuffling in her pink bunny slippers.

"Oh, my where is the coffee," she purred. "What on earth are you up so early for anyway?"

"I'm off with the kids to check out some stock on the north range. They have some doctor duties to attend too, I will be reading the tags on some live stock to take home. This is wonderful but I'm really anxious to get back home and get into the swing of things again."

"Well, you're right about the wonderful part, I could do this forever, however I'm sure our welcome would diminish by the day or maybe the hour. I will go for a ride on a horse, go for a swim, go on a tour of the security building. Watch the truck with new lambs come in and unload. Watch Tad cook and try to sneak some of his recipes. Roy just don't stay out in the sun too long and be sure and wear sun screen. Drink lots of water. Your brain needs to be hydrated to work at its optimal."

"Yep, I get it, I'm starting with this fresh squeezed orange juice and a mug of this incredible coffee. Followed up by scrambled eggs, bacon, hashbrowns, and toast. Yummy."

"Ok, that's enough of that. My mouth is already watering. You're just torturing me now."

Kyle and Molly slowly worked their way in and acknowledged everyone's presence.

"Mom who is that man over there shoving food into his face like he's never seen it before," chuckled a blurry eyed Molly.

"It's the wonder dad, can't you see that, he's survived a plane crash, a tornado sucking him into the atmosphere, being thrown off a merchant ship and, what is it now, twelve surgeries. Wonder dad, it's a wonder he's alive.

He's either the luckiest man alive or the unluckiest. I mean what are the odds, get sucked up by a tornado and tossed around suspended in the air, fly five or more miles, and then land in an 18-wheeler stock trailer full of sheep. It's a toss-up," said a cheeky Kyle.

"Well," said Ballard as he enters the room. "I think the key word in your little speech is the word...ALIVE. Anyone that can go through heck and high water, and survive, will have lots of stories to tell."

"OK all," said Gretchen. "Let's roll out, we've got work to do."

Pike and Scout were hot on her trail. Ralph and Molly loaded into one UV, Kyle and Gretchen the other. RJ would ride out in a SUV loaded with wranglers.

"Why all the wranglers today?" asked Roy to the driver.

"We had a fresh load of rodeo bulls delivered this week. One of them escaped the pen last night and is out roaming this part of the property. We are going to keep an eye out while you do your business. We have each got an air rifle with tranquilizer darts.

We also have one guy with a high-powered rifle in case the tranquilizers don't work fast enough to prevent a disaster. It will be a tragedy to lose a bull, unacceptable to lose a people. We'll keep watch while you pick your stock from the herd.

The vets are out looking for calves and or injured stock. If they find an animal that is deceased or diseased we call in the carcass disposal truck. We can't leave them out here, they attract predators. We work hard to keep the predators at a safe distance from stock. Dead or injured animals are a very unhealthy attraction.

We respect the wildlife, sometimes the wildlife doesn't respect us and our livelihoods. Carry on RJ, we're here."

They unloaded and started walking the herd. RJ had a scanner in hand and selected twenty-five head. The bull stayed away and all the animals were healthy. The llamas and donkeys were doing a great job of guard duty. The electronic countermeasure that faced away from the herd on the fence line triggered when there was motion detected. All good, safe and sound for another day.

"Did you find what you needed?" asked Clay.

"Sure did, they're a good-looking bunch of animals. I will send my stock trailer down to pick them up by the end of next week. What's that under your arm?"

"This is a gift to you from me and Lisa. His name is Rex. He's a ten-week-old pure breed German Shepherd pup. He's all yours."

"Oh my, come here buddy. He's adorable. Has Cherry seen him?"

"She picked him out of the litter just for you, RJ."

"Oh wow, he is beautiful. I don't know what to say. Thank you so much."

They went inside and found some lunch on the buffet ready to eat. They filled their plates and went out under the awning on the patio.

"Sweet tea on tap, who would have ever thought of that," said a cheerful RJ.

Rex galloped around the patio, sniffing at everything and dragging an old shoe around.

"Oh, I've got to get him through the chewing stage or Cherry will put us both out in the barn. Come here Rex."

The dog's ears perked up; RJ called his name again. He got his attention. Rex slowly crept over to RJ and sat at his feet. Of course, the smoked bologna was more than a bit of bait.

"We'll be checking out in the morning Clay. I need to get back. I've a ton of work to do around the property. Cherry kept it up pretty well, but it needs a coat of paint, new roof, fencing, sod in the yard. The usual stuff. I've got to make sure the corrals and perimeter fences are stable. It has been great to see you and Lisa. I still need to see that Security operation in action tonight."

"Sure thing, Roy," said Ballard. "Right after dinner we'll head over there. Oh, you might be interested to know this little secret. Molly and Skip, one of my security operators are flirting with each other pretty strongly. I just didn't want you to be surprised. It hasn't gone any further than the flirting stage. She is still committed to finishing her schooling before starting a serious relationship."

RJ, chuckled. "Well, she is a bit of magnet. A lot like her mom was at that age. Does Cherry know?"

"Yes, she does. She thinks Molly can handle herself. If she needs guidance she knows where to go."

"Tad, that was a wonderful dinner as usual," remarked RJ. Cherry and the kids all echoed their approval. "You do have a rival though. Our niece Mandy is a world class chef as well. She's taken over the Lazy J restaurant and event center in Pine Creek. The place stays busy all the time. Even we have to get a reservation."

Tad smiled, "I would love to meet her sometime and challenge her to a barbecue duel."

"We'll see if we can make that happen someday soon."

"Ok, guys anyone going up to the Security Center. Let's load up in the Bus."

They traveled the short distance up the hill to the Center. The sign 'Sky Hawks' over the door way, greeted them.

Ballard scanned them in. They walked into the first room where Skip and Quinn were watching the herds and the perimeters closely.

"Say there, Skip, how are those Mark 19 drones doing?"

"Hello sir, the Mark 19 has booted battery life by a factor of 5x. The scanning rates are double the previous model. The camera pixel rates are substantially higher. We can tell the difference between a cow, a horse, a bear, wolf, puma, and a cluster of monkeys, I mean humans. I was joking about the monkeys."

"That's great, in my early life a cluster of monkeys clogged up my Starscope something fierce. I was determined to get the technology together to tell them apart. I want to be able to name them one by one, ya' feel me!"

"Yes sir, I do," said Skip.

"If you have any ideas for improvement let my factory customer service team know. OK!"

"Yes sir,"

"Can we go in the other room now Clay?"

"Sure," said Ballard.

He scanned them into the next room.

RJ went in and drank in the screens that spanned the respective hemispheres.

"That is something else. My question of this group is. DID YOU GET HIM?"

"Yes sir, Dr. Jansen we got him and billions of his ill-gotten assets. The US State Department, Mr. Baker and his team are working to put all the displaced people back where they belong and distribute the monies to affected parties. There were so many people who were extorted or kidnapped, from all over the world, it's staggering.

Baker says it's a multibillion-dollar business now, trafficking people both in and out of the US and other countries. What you did on that RORO ship was the bravest thing we've ever seen."

"What I saw, how people were being swindled or treated so badly angered me to the pit of my soul. I had to do whatever I could to stop it. I'm glad I was able to help, I only hope it was enough."

"It was enough for now," said Ballard. "Others will need to carry the baton from now on. You've done your part."

"The cloaking device, it was supposed to be used by friendly forces. Did anyone figure out how Conners got ahold of it?"

"Yes," said Ballard. "That leak has been plugged permanently."

"That reminds me, I need to send Alex in Panama my heartfelt thanks for getting me turned around in the right direction. Do you guys have his phone number handy? I'd like to drop him a line."

"Dialing," said the Lead Operative.

"Hello Alex, this is Dave in Ops. How ya doing today?"

"Hello Dave, I'm great, to what do I owe the pleasure?"

"There's someone here that wants to say hello."

"Alex, RJ here, I wanted to phone and say how much I enjoyed our accidental rendezvous in Panama and to thank you for getting me headed in the right direction. You were instrumental in saving not only my life but the lives of hundreds of others and helping bring down a criminal master mind."

"It was good to see you RJ. I'm glad you made it home ok. It was pretty touch and go there for a while. Give Cherry my best and tell Ballard he owes me for some Bug Spray, I'm running really low since the Rangers have moved on. Alex out."

"RJ out, have a good one my friend."

They returned back to the ranch house and settled down for a few minutes before turning in. Roy sat between Kyle and Molly and held their hands.

"I want you guys to know how much you mean to me; thoughts of you guys are what helped me get through the hardest parts. I might not have known at the time everyone's name but I had a strong image of each of you in my head and heart.

I know you are each getting ready to enter your senior year at university. Whatever path you choose, I know you will choose wisely. Come home as soon as you can. We can go and play some golf at that new course up at Cyan Mountain. I've been working on my short game. I might break 110 this time. Good night kids. We are taking off early in the morning so we might not get to see you again this trip. Be safe and smart. I love you.

Come on Rex, let's hit the rack, you too, babe. Let's get some shut eye."

The next morning Cherry, Roy and baby Rex packed up and went downstairs. They grabbed a quick breakfast and coffee and hit the road.

"What do you plan on doing when we get home Roy?" Cherry asked.

"I've got a bunch of chores to catch up on. You did a good job keeping the place up. It's time for a spit shine though. New roof for starters. New landscaping. New paint. Mending all the fences to get ready for the new herd. I've got plenty to do. I need to work the physical therapy pretty hard, work out some of the kinks and adhesions. How about you sweetheart? What are you up to these days?"

"I'm working with the college of medicine on some experimental cancer detection and treatments. I really hope this new protocol is a game changer, especially for those affected by environmental toxins."

They got home early evening, unloaded, went and picked Sammy up from Dan and Martha's, and introduced her to baby Rex. At first, they were suspicious of one another. After a brief tussle, Sammy showed Rex who's boss.

"Ok guys, how about a trip to the Lazy J for dinner. We haven't been shopping lately so let's go get something hot and fresh."

They all jumped in the truck and drove over to the Lazy J. Dan and Martha soon joined them.

"Hey who is this that just walked in? said Mandy. Is that the Baby Rex we've heard so much about. Oh, how precious, he's adorable. Come here boy give us a hug. You too Uncle Roy. First time I've seen you awake in over three years. Let me look at you. You could use a spa treatment for that skin ailment."

"I know just the place," said Martha.

Dan just chuckled, "Good to see you son. Your mother is in rare form tonight.

How are you guys? How's Ballard and Lisa? Kyle and Molly?"

"There all good, getting reacquainted has been interesting. What's good for dinner tonight? I'm just going to put the pups outside in the play area."

"Ribeye's are really good, nice and tender. If you want roast chicken Mandy has a really nice recipe for that. Pot roast is always good, and don't forget to top it with her special apple pie."

"I think I'll have the ribeye and a baked potato, what about you Cherry?"

"The pot roast sounds really good to me; I think I'll have that."

"While we're waiting, I'm thinking about getting with Lanora's legal team to establish our property and assets in a trust with the kids as beneficiary's. Just in case anything else weird ever happens. Cherry will of course be first executor. The trust will only kick in if we are both incapacitated.

My will is going to state that our property must never be sold to anyone on cousin Dickie's side of the family. That weasel has been nosing around the property harassing Cherry to sell ever since I disappeared. He is the worst form of snake there is on the planet.

Anyway, I wanted to run all this by you for your opinion. Cherry and I have discussed it at length. Since what we've been through of late, if there's anything I've learned it's that anything can happen to anyone, anytime."

"Smart move son, your mother and I established a trust ages ago. We just don't advertise it."

"Good, that's settled then. Let us dig into this wonderful meal."

"Keep some leftovers for the pups."

The next day, Roy was surveying the needs of the property and getting contacts for the improvements. Standing in the drive looking back toward the house making a list of his requirements. Just then he heard a car roll up. He heard footsteps coming up behind him.

"Hey you, what are you doing here?" bellowed a deep voice, or of someone trying to sound like they had a deep voice.

Roy turned to face the man.

"Oh, ah, oops, a, a, hey man, Roy is that you? I thought you were a goner. I was just coming to check on whether or not Cherry was finally going to sell the property to me."

"Yes," hissed a very perturbed RJ. "It's me, kindly remove yourself and your vehicle off my property, and stay off. GOT IT! If I ever see you within a hundred yards of this place I will be filing trespassing charges on you, you RAT, how dare you come here and try to take advantage of my wife. GET!"

"Yeah, a, yeah Roy, I got it. I'm out a here."

Cousin Dickie smoked the tires backing up. He swerved out onto the highway.

Cherry came to the door and chuckled.

"Got rid of him huh," she said.

"The nerve of that guy. He was always trying to weasel me out of stuff. He even tried to trick me into selling the Cherry-1 before I went into the Airforce.

"Yes, he's been a thorn for a while now. He had that coming. I've been avoiding him at all costs. I bet he will leave me, us, alone now," said Cherry.

The home improvements underway, Roy was pleased with the progress.

"When it's all done, we need to have a big shindig, ok Cherry," said RJ.

"I've not seen Douglas or his new wife lately, or Tom and Marsha. We need to get them over for a weekend. Maybe we can time that to just before the kids go back to school for the fall semester. What do you think?"

"Sounds good to me, since you're doing all the cooking and cleaning. I'm all in," she said with a laugh.

Chapter Sixteen

"RJ's Diary"

My therapist told me that journaling, or as I call it, writing things down, is good for helping me remember things, not good or bad, just things.

I was writing yesterday when I suddenly realized that I had missed three birthday's, three anniversary's, Christmas's, and so on. Not mine, Cherry's. So, I got on the internet and bought several dozen red and yellow roses and they just showed up right after I ordered them. This new part of the internet is very interesting. You can order stuff and it shows up. For a price mind you. I can think of all kinds of things I can order.

Cherry was amazed and thought I had gone to a lot of work to get the flowers. I'll not tell her my secret just yet. Maybe when the new furniture shows up and she knows I can't drive yet.

Speaking of driving, I got clearance from Clarence the head PT guy, to start driving today. I'm so excited. I plan on taking the stingray out for a spin later.

It's now tomorrow. I can drive so I went over to the electronics plant and met with the design team about building some high powered invisible light lasers for voice and visual communications. We started working on the schematics and getting the parts procured for a prototype. I also want a laser that scans tornadoes for speed, direction, velocity and what else is going on inside the things.

I swear when I was in the air flying around, just before I blacked out, hard stuff, like trees and metal stuff was flying around with me and some of it was bending and twisting and then all of a sudden it would snap back into place. I think that would explain the straw in the tree thing, basically the tree opens up and invites it in and then shuts down making it look like the wind blew it in, well it did, sort of. It would also explain the nail in the magnesium wheel thing where it looks like the nail was a part of the wheel, the wheels molecules vibrated violently turning to a gel sort of and then the nail just found its way in. It could also explain how a windshield wiper could go through a windshield and literally become a fixture of the windshield without as much a micro crack in the glass.

Anyway, I want to build a laser that can scan a tornado from a distance and really see what is going on inside one of those devils. There is a lot more going on in there than just the wind blowing around. That might be a chore but I bet with some ingenuity I can figure that out.

I went over to the lab at the college where Dr. Cook and Sally his trusty assistant and now wife work on all sorts of projects. He was working on the effect on human cells with exposure to different types of laser light and power.

Sally had invited me over to visit them. It had been quite a while since we had seen each other. She privately had come up with a joke to play on Alfred, Dr. Cook. He still has that Time Machine sitting in the lab. He plays with it now and then; she's always tricking him with it.

She had me come into the lab and casually mention in passing that it sure would be nice to go back in time and maybe drive a different direction sometime in May 99. He had his head down and was otherwise engaged in some experiment. I walked over to the machine and fooled around with the knobs while Sally flipped on the switch in the back and it fired up and bright lights flashed and there was an explosion of smoke and noise.

I snuck off in the confusion while Alfred was screaming, "Don't touch that Dial."

Sally stuck a watermelon on the seat in the machine. When the smoke cleared Alfred screamed, "RJ, you've turned into a watermelon."

In a few minutes I came walking back in just like before and pretended like I had been off on an adventure. Sally is laughing her head off in the corner office. Alfred had the most puzzled look on his face. He finally figured out she had been playing jokes on him all along.

"It's great to see you RJ." He told me.

We had a good laugh and shared information on a new project we could both work on.

It's tomorrow again. Baby Rex is getting his adult voice and wants to bark at every passing motorist. He scared the mailman half to death yesterday. We will be doing some training in the next few weeks to get that behavior under control. Little Sammy finally curled up in my lap and took a nap while I watched golf on TV. I didn't know you could do that until recently after installing satellite dishes all over Central America.

We're getting ready for the big, end of summer shindig here at the house. All the fixings are ordered and received. The house looks great, new roof, paint, grass in the yard. The new stock arrived and are grazing in the field. I got us a donkey for protection from predators. His name is...DONKEY.

The kids have been back from Ballard's for the past few days. Everyone is coming, Douglas and his bride Nancy. Tom and Marsha. Speaking of Tom and Marsha, they seem to have slowed down a bit, rumor has it that she might be expecting sometime in December.

Dan and Martha are here of course. Dan says he has a big announcement to make. I'm seriously curious what that might be. They've been traveling a lot in their retirement, who knows, maybe they want to move to Florida or something.

Lanora and Darren are here, they are doing really well. Their daughters Mandy and Lea are professionals and are attracting lots of good attention, suitors are lining up to take their chances. Lea made it to the Kansas City station and is doing an expose on the mythical 'SKY MAN' while Mandy is winning star after star with her restaurant business.

Cherry is working on new techniques to treat pediatric cancer and other childhood diseases.

Even Jeb and Jane the grand parents are going to be here. They are in their nineties now and don't get out much. I go over and visit regularly. Pops helps me recall important events in history. I will tell you though the phrase "Remember When," is getting a bit tired. I will live with and through it with a smile on my face. Pops is the best; Grandma is the heart and soul of the family though.

It's tomorrow again. Today is the day of the big shindig. I've got everything I need to make it a barbecue for the ages. Signing off for now. Until it's tomorrow again.

Chapter Seventeen

"Don't Touch that Dial"

"Thanks everyone for coming, this has been a real treat. It's been a while since we were all together. I trust everyone has caught up on everyone else's news. It's such a thrill to have RJ back in one piece. Well, his pieces are at least in one place.

Today I want to invite you on another one of our family vacations. This is a big one, you will see what I mean when I detail it out.

We, the entire family has been invited to attend an episode of the Carson show in Hollywood California, RJ, aka SKY MAN has been requested by them to be a guest on the show. Everyone is interested in how everything turned out for SKY MAN after his Central American adventures.

The show is schedule for two weeks from now. It is an expense paid trip for all of us that want to attend. In addition, we will be going to visit all of the theme parks, the beach, the pier, you name it. I personally want to visit Catalina Island and scope out the Pelicans.

Are you all excited, I see stunned faces in the crowd. All in?" asked Dan.

There was a huge chorus of, "Yeah hoo."

Everyone, get your traveling clothes ready for a week in California. Don't forget to pack some fancy duds for the TV show. I will make the flight arrangements for everyone."

"How in the world did you pull that off, Dad," said a dazed RJ. "Do I have to make a speech or something?"

"No just be you, he will ask you some questions, that's all."

The family gathered at the Kansas City airport. Jeb and Jane opted to watch the show on TV. The flight was uneventful the transitions were smooth as glass. They had hotel reservations on the beach in Malibu.

Cherry popped open the drapes on the room and exposed it to a bath of glorious sunlight.

"I'm a little bit nervous about this honey," remarked RJ.

"Oh, gosh, you will be just fine. Let that Jansen sense of humor loose, you will be fine."

Dan went over to the studio to meet with Ms. Carpenter.

"Everything ready Mr. Jansen?" said Ms. Carpenter.

"Oh, you can call me Dan. Yeah, the gang is all here. RJ is alive and well and just a little nervous. I think he will settle as soon as it gets started."

"I bet he will be just fine. Will he be here soon? The staff wants to meet him before we go on. Jonny, Ed and Doc will all be here too in a few minutes."

"Here he comes now. RJ this is Ms. Carpenter, she is the producer of the show and the arranger of this event tonight."

"Nice to meet you, Ms. Carpenter."

The staff filed into the conference room and chatted for a few minutes. Jonny, Ed and Doc came in and the jokes started reeling out.

"So, Mr. or should I say Dr. Jansen. Your reputation as SKY MAN has exploded worldwide. People everywhere on Earth want to see you in person, or at least on the small screen."

"I'm here, at your service. Ask your questions."

"Oh, we pretty much know everything there is to know about you already. I will ask you some questions so the studio and viewing audience can get to know you."

"Ok, folks, see you at five o'clock sharp," said Ms. Carpenter.

The whole family had front row seats and filed in and sat down. Watching with wide eyes the whole process.

RJ was back stage waiting to be called out.

"Hello, everyone in TV land and all you inhabitants of the studio tonight. How's it going tonight, Ed, are you excited to meet our first guest?"

"Sure am, I plan to negotiate with him for a satellite dish with 247 channels."

"How about you Doc?"

"Oh yeah, he's going to play along with us on his twelve-string guitar a resounding rendition of Happy Trails. Hoo rah."

After the break we will bring out 'SKY MAN' as he was affectionately dubbed, let's get this party started.

There was a brief commercial break, when it was over Jonny called RJ out to the stage.

RJ waved to everyone and blew a kiss to Cherry sitting in the front row.

"Hello there SKY MAN, or Dr. Jansen in real life.

How on earth did you wind up in that trailer with a bunch of sheep? And what are the odds that a person flung up in the air and suspended floating for over five miles would land in a trailer full of sheep."

"I was in the right place at the wrong time Jonny. I mean, I wasn't counting them or anything but they did provide a very soft landing."

"I've never met anyone that has been inside a tornado and lived to talk about it. It's all fascinating to me. So, you were found, hospitalized with many injuries, they fixed you up but you had no memory of who you were or where you were from. How did you wind up with the new name Roy Rogers? Oh, is that the famous wrist watch there on your arm? Hold it up for the studio audience to see. Get a close up of that, camera man. That is so fascinating."

"Well Jonny as it turns out that is my real name. My name is...Roy Rogers Jansen."

"What, well that is just so cool. What do you think Ed?"

"As long as I get my satellite dish you can call him Jimmy Cricket." Audience laughter.

"Well that explains a lot," said an amused Doc.

"So, you went around putting up satellite dishes for all those people down there. What was that like?"

"I needed something to keep me busy after I was able to move around. I found some pieces of a dish and started playing around with it. Next thing I know I've got a dish receiving no less than 247 channels. It really caught on. Those folks really love their football down there."

The resources would just appear out of nowhere and I would get busy and fix up a feed and a dish. Worked my way down to Belize City when I got invited very strongly to go aboard a RORO ship and work as an electronics mate."

"What's a RORO ship for our audience?"

"It's a roll on roll off ship, carrying vehicle cargo."

You made it to Panama where you ran into an old friend and he sparked your memory and you started the journey home. Got back on the ship and low and behold when they were done with you, they tossed you overboard. We here heard you were done for. It was a sad day.

Imagine the excitement around here when we found out you were alive. I will say we got lots of mileage off your adventures. So, are you fully healed now? I mean is your memory all back?"

RJ froze for a moment looking glassy eyed and stunned...everyone gasped.

"Yeah, I'm fine, I was just messing with ya'. I even remember my third-grade teacher's name. Elenor something.

Just then RJ looked up and stuttered for just a second. He whispered to himself, "I'll be, there is Bud Conley in the audience right behind Cherry.

"Ok then, RJ, or Roy Rogers Jansen you have your guitar with you and you are going to play along with a rendition of Happy Trails with the orchestra, go on over there and hook up."

"Thanks, Jonny, for having us, Ed, my electronics team is installing your satellite dish as we speak, Doc yours is on the way tomorrow. If you want one Jonny we will hook you up as well."

"Ed, ED, get a hold of yourself man. He's over there sobbing into his handkerchief again. Fire it up Doc."

The orchestra kicked in the tune for Happy Trails.

RJ sang along..." Happy Trails to you everyone, until we meet again."

"DON'T touch that Dial folks...we'll be right back after these commercial messages."

Whistles, yells and loud applause...from the audience!

Author's Notes

Weather safety is no laughing matter. I personally suffered a broken back, dislocated pelvis, shoulders, neck, and a concussion with mild memory loss after an encounter with an F-3 tornado in June of 1998. That event resulted in a spinal fusion and hip replacements. Myself and my family witnessed first-hand what it was like to be inside the funnel of a tornado.

On the ground between automobiles in a parking lot with no warning of any kind. We hunkered down against an embankment and watched as the violent storm passed directly over us. The multi vortex funnel bracketed us, one vortex missed us on the south by about fifteen yards, the other to the north of us by about the same. We were extremely blessed as trees were flying like twigs and metal like paper. Power lines broken and sagging just missed us as we laid on the ground waiting for it to pass.

It was both terrifying and fascinating at the same time. The thunderous roar of the wind as it approached and the violent hiss of the static electricity as it departed. We watched as solid objects twisted and morphed into unrecognizable shapes and then just as suddenly snapped back into shape.

We live by the grace of God. We lived that day by his Grace and his hand of love over us. AMEN

Did you love *Outbreak on the Plains*? Then you should read *Mystery Of The Mist At Cyan Mountain*[1] by T. J. Judah!

[2]

After their exploits in 'Cherry-1 A Combat Controllers Tale,' R.J. and Cherry are settling into normal life. He, in his engineering work at the electronics factory and She, at her children's clinic. They have one young son, Douglas.

The peace and tranquility of this relatively unknown and unassuming community was about to change with the shock wave of a single .22 caliber bullet shot into the side of an otherwise innocuous looking hillside.

No strangers to mysteries and challenges, the team of Jansen and Company must now unravel the 'Mystery of the Cyan Super Storm,' one that vaults them into a whole new arena of problem solving.

---

1. https://books2read.com/u/mdYlxZ

2. https://books2read.com/u/mdYlxZ

About the Author

The author served in the USAF in the early 1970's in the Tactical Air Command as an Avionics Maintenance Specialist-Airborne Navigational Aids Repairman. He met and married his sweetheart and have raised two daughters, with six grandchildren. The last ten years of his career he was a Management and Program Analysist for the Federal Aviation Administrations Flight Program Operations group.